Meeting Lives

Published by

NIYOGI BOOKS

D-78, Okhla Industrial Area, Phase-I
New Delhi-110 020, INDIA

Tel: 91-11-26816301, 26813350, 51, 52
Fax: 91-11-26810483, 26813830

email: niyogibooks@gmail.com
website: www.niyogibooks.com

Text © Tulsi Badrinath

Cover Painting: Buwa Shete, *Mother and Child*
Cover Design: Navidita Thapa

ISBN: 978-81-89738-38-9

Publication: November 2008

Printed at: Niyogi Offset Pvt. Ltd., New Delhi, India

Meeting Lives

Tulsi Badrinath

NIYOGI
BOOKS

Vagarthaviva samprktau vagarthapratipattaye
Jagatah pitrau vande parvatiparameshwarau.

To gain the right understanding of speech and its sense,
I bow to Parvati-Parameshwara, parents of the universe,
as inseparable as word from meaning.

—Kalidasa, *Raghuvamsa*

For Parvati and Parameshwara in my life,
my parents Seeta and Chaturvedi Badrinath,
who taught me the relation between word and meaning
in their own distinctly individual ways.

Nectar in the ear

'Wake up, my child,
the morning has come;
and live O Krishna,
for a hundred, hundred autumns.'
Thus was he addressed
by Yashoda
and his face
for long beheld by her.
Him do we worship.

— *Krishna-karnamritam, II.67*

That divinity abiding in every being in the form of illusion,
I bow my head before Her, again and again and again
and yet again.

The skin submits with reluctant grace to the unbearable weight of cloth; summer has begun. It is an afternoon in April. I stand by a window in my room, the window that gives onto the garden and to the street beyond, and see Thayee framed by the dusty leaves of the mango tree.

She seems small due to the strange magic wrought by perspective on height and distance, smaller than she really is, seems the same size as this star-shaped bunch of leaves brushing the window. As the dark green bough sways, she is wholly visible, then covered over, then seen in part through the foliage, now the brown weather-beaten limbs, now the grey matted hair, stiff about her shrivelled face.

So much is she a part of what presents itself to the eye — green thatched against the sky, rough bark and shadows fallen to dry ground — it does not seem odd that she should be there, living out the end of her life on that bit of sun-warmed earth, the tiny neem flowers falling like white raindrops on her.

Often, when I pass her on the street, I notice two or three of those dainty flowers resting in her hair. They lend her an oddly youthful appearance, that of a wizened nymph perhaps. She gathers her hair into a rough knot, and fashions a turban out of rags, sprinkling water on the once white cloth before placing it on her head. Lately, she has settled herself near the gates of the house opposite. The widow who owns it goes abroad for long stretches of time and Thayee has free access to the grounds of that property. But then Thayee makes her way in and out of all our gardens, and, to this day, no one has been able to deter her.

Beside her, on the ground is a pile of dried coconut leaves. In two swift, practised movements, she tears the sword-like body of a long leaf and the spine emerges—clean, distinct, golden-brown. Calmly, she strips one, then another, a third, and in a while, the heap is reduced to a tangled mass of dead leaf. To the right, near her knees, the thin, flexible spines nestle together, waiting to be tied with a string and given a new collective identity.

The sea breeze has set in, running its fingers through the long hair of the coconut trees. A squirrel races down the tree on the left and up another, squeaking in its high-pitched, excited way and then suddenly stops, poised in delicate indecision on the sloping trunk. Thayee lies on her side in the healing shade of the neem and falls asleep. Above her, a multi-layered canopy of leaves sifts imperfectly the blaze of sunlight; her toes slip in and out of a waver of gold. I run my hand across the back of my neck and wipe it on my kurta.

A fierce longing surges within me; the recurring torment of desire. When will I dance again? When will I embark on that familiar journey on stage, exploring a universe of space to the measure of time? The energy that once impelled my dancing feet has been abruptly stilled... Panic seizes my heart: *I must dance, I must, I must...*

I enter the memory of a performance, feel the heat of the lights on my body draped in silk, the golden space that is my own, private, personal, yet shared with a large audience.

I tear my mind away from that whirling image of a bejewelled dancer, me, and return to Thayee.

I have begun to watch her these days, just as I have begun to stare out of my window at odd times of the day and the night, waiting for life to happen. Sometimes, she is not there and yet the signs, unmistakable as they are, speak of her occupation of that sandy strip of ground edging the tarred road: a faded blue bucket, an empty paint can in which she stores water, a bundle of unstitched greyish cloth, and a piece of cardboard, part of the larger packaging in which an air conditioner had arrived. I look through the gaps within the leaves, and for a moment, I think I see her — the rounded fold of a dusty garment, the slim, brown branch of the tree, her bare arm perhaps — but I am mistaken.

This awareness of her has come to me gradually, gaining depth in the recent past, although it has been quite some time, six years at least, since she moved her things out of our garden onto the street. Perhaps the time she hoarded garbage in our garden was when I first took notice of her, recognising in her an astonishing, obdurate strength that had managed, temporarily, to vanquish Amma, my mother.

On one side, the space between our house and the compound wall is just about the mandatory five feet. We rarely use that corridor of land, something that Thayee discovered fairly quickly. A wasted, secure space where she could store some of her things — to her mind, it was as simple as that. She opened the gate, dragged an enormous polythene bag across the lawn and installed it between the tap and the drumstick tree. There it was discovered by Amma on a Sunday when she was watering the garden. I don't know what Amma said to her or even how she knew it was Thayee's but to my surprise, Thayee was allowed to keep her possessions there on the condition that they were arranged neatly in a way that they were not visible from either the gate or the house.

Around this time a thief visited our house twice — on two successive nights.

We then began the elaborate locking-up routine that we follow each night. We slept with the windows latched and the curtains resolutely drawn all through summer and we could never rid ourselves of the thought that in the darkness outside crouched a man, his eyes intent on us as we moved around, or ate or slept.

After a while, it became too much of an effort to open in the day time those windows that looked onto the bare, narrow corridor and to shut them at night; the view did not afford an equal pleasure. So, the windows remained closed, the curtains drawn, and spiders spun their fine webs in the curved spaces between the grills.

All this was to Thayee's advantage. The passage was hers, the window ledge hers, Amma being the only intruder who ventured there every now and then to water the ashoka and the drumstick trees. Once, I lifted the curtain absentmindedly and found a host of ghostly shapes scrabbling against the glass panes, clamouring to be let in. Things continued this way and so they would have had Thayee had not become over-ambitious.

In June that year, Amma went to Bangalore for a month. I was given instructions, extremely complicated ones, about locks and keys and packets of milk and the storing of water, my father's medicines and supervising the maid — most of which I neglected to follow until the day of her return.

'All part of your training,' she had said, a humorous gleam in her eyes, 'next year, this time you will be running your own home. Imagine!'

Thayee had stored a good harvest in the unused passage, and when the heat became worse, she stopped her rounds.

One day, she decided to sort and grade her pickings. For this, she needed space. One after another, she lugged the plastic bags from safety into the open and spread their contents like a richly patterned carpet on the lawn.

There, seated on the dew-moistened grass, her short legs stretched out in front of her, she smoothened out crumpled newspapers, arranged empty beer bottles in intricate designs of brown and white, built a smelly translucent tower with empty milk sachets and culled bits and pieces of metal from a heap of indistinguishable objects.

I rather liked the sight of the glorious anarchy on the grass that Thayee had created with impunity, something that even I, Amma's only child, would have hesitated to attempt.

Standing, unnoticed by her, to one side of the lawn, I watched her for a while. Then, when I informed her of Amma's impending return, she lifted her head slowly, looked at me in her blank, unseeing way and said, 'Aatom, aatom,' dismissing the news and my unspoken order without a pause in her labour.

The next morning, I locked every cupboard I could think of, filled the tank until it began to overflow, rescued some plants that were dying on the balcony upstairs and hid them behind the well, threw away the mouldy vegetables in the fridge and managed to give back to the house some of its crisp, straight-edged order, but Thayee had not cleared up her formidable collection of paper and plastic.

Amma arrived just before noon.

I waited.

She took a bath and wandered into the garden. Snapping a wayward branch here, a cheeky leaf there, she reached the lawn and then, she screamed. I ran towards her, giggling. She was kneeling near a cutting of jasmine, its drooping head cradled in her palm.

'I don't believe this. You see what I told you? These people—give them an inch and they...my lawn, my lovely lawn. She's trampled all over my plants, killed half of them. Enough is enough! She will have to remove this junk *now*. She can't use our lawn as a shop, a junkyard. She may start living here, or move in permanently. Soon I'll have to wait on her hand and foot. Who knows what next?'

Reality is just too drab for Amma; she must dress it in vivid colours. By evening, Thayee had repacked her wealth and dragged it, bag by bag, three houses away.

The windows were opened that day, the cobwebs smashed with a duster, the curtains changed and we realised that we had forgotten how airy and bright the room really was in the days before the arrival of the thief.

So much has come to pass since then. I made a name for myself as a dancer, got married, went away, had a baby, then returned home, and suddenly, without warning, time acquired a different dimension.

One day blurs into the next. A year has the semblance of eternity, an endless tunnel with no visible light.

The 'I' that speaks of Thayee now, is a different one. It sees a human being who simply tells the time of day by looking at the sun; it sees a life that leans against nothing for support and yet survives.

Sanju races into the room. Flinging his arms around me, he clambers up and settles himself on my hip. He pulls my head low and gives me a kiss. There is jam on my cheek and hair.

The 'I' that speaks of Thayee is a newborn, an unfamiliar creature — one-and-a-half people — a mother and a child, conjoined at the hip.

~

Around four thirty in the afternoon, when the sun relents a little, the street is transformed by children. Three sticks held upright by a heap of sand; a boundary drawn with a piece of brick, red against the black of tar; a rubber ball, and the long, rectangular road becomes both pitch and field. Each time a vehicle turns around the corner, the stumps are dismantled and the players troop raggedly to the side. Their game lasts only as long as the boy who owns the bat is present. When he leaves, the others fall silent, purposeless all of a sudden.

I throw the frisbee and Sanju runs to catch it, his arms outstretched. It comes to me then, the thought that in this group of shouting, adolescent boys, the two excited girls there, wobbling on a gent's cycle, and further away in that pulsing knot of very young children, some with bright ribbons in their hair, are Thayee's grandchildren.

They ignore her in their play, shun her at all times.

Above us, birds fly in perfect unison, like a huge, silver arrowhead speeding towards the river while the reddish-orange glow fades from the sky. Gradually, almost imperceptibly, the children disappear, and the street is restored to its former, less noisy state. Even Sanju tires of play; we walk home.

When we are close enough for her to see us, Thayee folds her hands before him in greeting, '*Vanakam-ayya*,' and smiles mischievously, her lips parted to reveal a dark, toothless cave. Seated this way—her knees drawn up to her chest—she is of the same height as he is. Sanju, who is five years old, is fond of her and of all those who make up his small, often puzzling universe. Amused by her ignorance of his name, he says, 'Look, she calls me *vanakam-ayya!*' Then, liking the word, he repeats it, '*Vanakam-ayya, vanakam-ayya*,' and dances around her like a boxer, for he can never keep still.

Later, as we pass through the gate, he asks, 'Maa, why does Thayee sleep on mud?' and I hesitate, troubled, fiercely reluctant to create this aspect of the world for him.

~

He stirs.

Is it time already? Maybe he will sleep a little while longer.

Must the day begin now? Tiredness weighs me down; sleep does not grant a complete respite it seems. A tiny finger pokes about my shut eyelids, trying to prise them open.

'Maa,' he says. 'Maa, wake up. Monning. Monning come.' I cuddle him, but he wriggles free of me. It is just six thirty. He must not leave the room; he will wake everyone up. Sanju jumps up and down, trying to reach the latch on the door. It is placed high, beyond his reach. Fortunately, he finds a toy helicopter near the bed and picks it up. I drift back into an uncomfortable sleep. I am smashing something against the floor, hitting it hard, resolutely. It must yield.

Crash! It's broken.

I sit bolt upright on the bed.

Is he okay? He is. Surrounding him are the remains of the helicopter, a cracked plastic fuselage, dangerous screws, a decapitated pilot and a wheel that is spinning endlessly.

'Naughty boy! Why did you break it?' My eyes feel sandy.

He looks at me in incomprehension: *Why shouldn't it be broken?* How else would he know how it works? Besides, even after it had come apart, he couldn't really tell how it worked…

Tears of frustration roll down his cheeks.

Finally, it's time for breakfast. I break off a piece of steaming idli, blow on it, dip it in sugar and place it in his mouth.

'Hot, hot!' he screams and spits it out. I have to blow on the next morsel at least ten times before he is satisfied. He opens his mouth and I pop it in. The food remains in his mouth. He fidgets with a toy car, running it up and down the table.

'Eat,' I say gently. 'Eat!'

After great persuasion, when he opens the mouth for the next bite, there is that ball of idli still tucked inside his left cheek.

'Just leave it,' says Appa, my father, exasperated by the scene. 'He will feel hungry and eat by himself.'

'He won't. He doesn't even *look* at food! I *know*, he will just become more and more cranky. He doesn't know that feeling in his tummy is hunger.'

Appa throws up his hands.

One hour later, when I start on my breakfast, Sanju yells for me. *'Potty aachu!'*

I rush to clean him. Strangely, his potty always smells of jasmine. I return to the table.

The idlis are cold and I have lost my appetite.

I give him a colouring book and crayons; they fail to interest him. I propose a jigsaw puzzle.

No.

I find some sketch pens and paper and he decides to draw a rocket. I leave him to put a load of clothes in the washing machine. When I get back, I find a green pool on the white mosaic floor.

The floor was more interesting to colour.

We embark on cleaning the green ink off the floor before Amma sees it.

He wants me to play ball with him and will not stop when I tire of the game. He is screaming now, flinging himself against me with all his weight. His voice is like a drill, boring a hole through my skull.

I realise he is hungry.

It seems ages since I woke up.

I place him in front of the computer. It's the only way to make him stay in one place while I feed him. He is busy making a tangram bridge on the screen. I hold a spoon of curd and rice to his mouth but he will not open it.

'Sanju!'

Startled, he turns suddenly and knocks the bowl over. Mashed rice coats the floor. Disrespect to food. Tears sting my eyes. There is no point in shouting. It tires me even more. I clean the mess off the floor, scatter it outside for the crows and return to mop the place. Then I mix some more curd and rice, and we start again.

My heart sinks to my feet, leaking out of me. I am in the grip of something larger than me and infinitely more powerful. It gives me only so much room to manoeuvre, and exults in my distress.

Afternoon.

I sling him across my body, settle his head on my shoulder. He insists on a story, told just the way he likes it, not one word to be left out. Slowly, the head gets heavier, settles itself one final time, and he is asleep. I sit on the bed and then lie down, sliding him onto the bed. The touchdown is critical. He starts. I press his limbs firmly and take a deep breath.

Sanju is quiet at last, his arms and legs exposed to a steady breeze from the fan. The hair on his forehead flutters, shining every now and then as it catches the light. The water lorry is late today. It grinds past the house, with its piercing siren. I am tense. Why can't the world tiptoe around his sleeping form as lightly as I do? A crow descends on the window ledge, cawing morosely. It will take just one extraordinary, amplified sound to wake him up. There is peace for a while. Then the itinerant cobbler arrives. He pauses near the hedge, beneath the window, calling '*Jodi ripeyr, jodi ripeyr*' loudly.

I could cry.

There is a conspiracy of sounds thereafter. Three stray dogs start fighting; one gets hurt and runs away yelping. The driver starts a conversation with somebody. A courier deliveryman rings the bell. Miraculously, Sanju does not transgress his dream.

When he wakes up from his nap, I am ready to forgive the world its noise.

In the evening, I bribe him with the idea of a visit to the beach. His tiffin vanishes marginally faster. We pack water, a snack, some toys, money, a change of clothes, paper napkins, and a towel before we leave. I, who scorned handbags, now carry a baggy holdall everywhere, fearful of being stranded without supplies.

On the way, he fidgets with the slats of the air vent on the side of the car. I cannot drive and supervise him at the same time. By the time we are at the beach, one of the slats has come off in his hand. He looks at me from the corner of his eyes and tries to put it back but cannot.

It is Wednesday. No, Tuesday. There are not many people on the beach at five in the evening. The sea is a foam-speckled line of blue in the distance, where the sky falls into the earth. Sanju responds with glee to the amplitude of sand: *room to run, room to release all that energy that courses through his body.* He runs in wider and wider circles. Then tiring, he sits next to me and begins to dig with a red spade.

'What'll happen if I keep digging and digging?'

'You'll make a tunnel to the middle of the earth.'

'Then what?'

'You'll reach a ver-*ry* hot place.'

'Then what?'

'That's all. You can't dig any more.'

'Then after that what?'

I give up, 'You'll reach the other side of the earth.'

He makes a passage to the Pacific and my mind wanders back to a distant past.

A discovery in the fourth-month results in an abridged wait: a five-month pregnancy. This being whose heart races like an express train over iron tracks, this being that is a part of me and yet distinct, is like a secret that will be shared, an enigma that will cease to exist simultaneously as the baby is born.

'A boy!'

There is barely enough time to absorb the sight of the naked baby, his face red from the exertion of crying, the black down that covers his shoulders, back and his pale flesh unacquainted with the sun, before he is borne away to be covered with clothes and civilisation. The nurses bathe him, dress his small body in pink smocking and wrap him up in a blanket while I lie exhausted, emptied, shivering uncontrollably.

Later, they place the warm cowled bundle in my arms.

I look down at the face of my baby. He is fair, like a piece of the moon, with seven eyelashes on each eyelid and a rash of white pimples on his nose. His nails have a sheen and have grown past the padded tips of his tiny fingers; I will have to trim them. He is sleeping, but those tiny fingers wrap themselves tightly around the tip of my index finger. Love and the weight of motherhood descend on me. I understand that I will never be the same again. This, more than marriage, has made a woman out of me.

My baby is three months old and I have left him for the first time, with Amma, in order to attend dance class at my guru's home. In the long rectangular hall, Sir is seated on a mat on the floor, calling out corrections even as he gives the beat with a simple wooden stick. I do not recognise a single face among the students practising, the girls wearing knee-length saris over pyjamas, the bare-chested boys in dhotis worn in a way that the cloth wraps around each leg, leaving it free for movement. Their bodies glisten with sweat.

Disconcerted and trembling from within, I enter the familiar room, step onto the expanse of the smooth stone floor, deliciously cool beneath my feet. My limbs are slow to move. Every movement seems wrong. Those years of discipline, of single-minded focus, allow me to reach the position, but a fraction of a second too late. I feel dizzy. My body, the supple instrument of dance, has changed. I carry the remnants of pregnancy on my swollen arms, my distended stomach. Where once I cut through space, I wade, I wobble. I feel clumsy and yet, a tiny voice within me is singing the ecstasy of movement: *I am back, I am back. I dance!*

My guru tells me that the troupe is going abroad in four months' time to perform the dance-drama *Ammaiyaar*. The lead role, that of Punitavati, is mine. Will I come, Sir asks, conferring this honour on me with a smile. I look at him, at the beloved face that I have watched since I was a child, gazing in wonder at the subtlety of the expressions flitting across his face. Just as I have seen him age from a young man, the lines of his handsome face softening, his hair gradually turning grey, he too has seen me grow from a talkative little eight-year-old girl into womanhood. I mull over his offer.

The thrill of a performance! Rehearsals, live music, the sound of the *veena*! I'll have to lose weight fast!

When the first rush of excitement recedes, I remember my baby. In an hour it will be time to feed him again. *How can I leave him and travel?* I am still his lifeline, his food supply. Once he grew inside me. Now he does so lying alongside, his hand spread like a flower against my left breast, taking hurried, greedy gulps of milk.

I've made a discovery. I understand what breasts are meant for. Their function is pure.

My guru hears my answer mumbled reluctantly, and turns away in disapproval. I leave the class just before the front of my blouse begins to get discoloured.

On the way out, I see incomprehension writ large on the faces of some of the younger dancers. I have said no to a trip to America, spurned the chance of a lifetime!

For a year, while I wean my baby, I give up the discipline of practice, *sadhana*.

My husband Murthy's life has not changed essentially. Mine has. The notion of equality and togetherness has ended with the offering from one side of sperm, and from the other, ovum. The entities of boy and father are not as different as those of girl and mother are.

He leaves for work, he pays the necessary, is an individual. I stay at home, become a stranger to myself and am alone in bringing up my child. If I were to paint a family portrait, it would be of me, Lata, the maid and the baby.

Then one day Murthy announces that he has been offered an assignment in France. It will last a year and he will be travelling a lot. There is no point in shifting the family for such a short period. The baby and I can stay with my parents. Since he has already decided all this on my behalf, there seems little point in arguing. Besides, I am attached to the maid.

A month later, when Lata leaves, my life comes apart. No maid since has been able to manage Sanju's wild energy; they leave within a week. I am now his cook, chauffeur, ayah, potty-cleaner, nurse, playmate and nourishing bully, all rolled into one.

'Maa!'

I return to the present with a jerk. Light crystallises into the yellow of the sand, the ice-blue of the sky and the infinite rainbow of women's saris; we are still at the beach.

'*Amma. Paaru Maa.* Look, I dug so much far. Bye!' He smiles. In an instant, he is up and bounding across the sand, away from me. The place is crowded now. Children play cricket and throwball. Old men dressed in white gather in a circle. People from land-locked villages make a pilgrimage to the sea, dressed in their festive best. There are vendors everywhere. If I lose sight of him, I'll never be able to find him in this crowd. He might get kidnapped!

I race after him but the shifting surface of sand draws my feet in, hampers me from moving faster.

'Sanju!'

The imp waits for me to catch up a little before he prances away, laughing all the while.

What joy, he is free! The world is so big, so interesting. He has never seen this part of the beach before. There is a cotton candy man, colourful balloons, flying horses with children on their backs...why didn't Maa show him all this earlier?

He runs steadily. I cannot run. I am getting slower, ponderous as an elephant. Now I can't see him; two men drift into my range of vision and drift out again. Something is squeezing my chest, forcing out the air. I will lose my child, never see him again. I have to stop for breath, fight the panic. A rush of relief— *there he is in the distance.* A teenager hears me shout. He looks up; I gesture frantically towards Sanju, and hold my palm in the stop position; 'Catch him,' I scream, but the wind carries my words in the other direction. The boy understands. His friends corral my son into the safety net of their hands and I stumble over a stone, thanking them all the while.

I slap him across his cheek, and am instantly sorry. The imprint of fingers is visible, four red bars welling on innocent skin. There is a look of disbelief on his face; his eyes go still. I gather him into my arms as he begins to cry. We walk back, his bottom resting on the saddle made of my hands. I need to feel every part of his little body through mine. I feel his hair tickling my cheek, his legs girdling my waist, feel the satisfying rhythm of his breath on my shoulder. I hug him close and am rendered sane. If he were gone, I would not be me.

I carry him the entire distance back to where we left our belongings, scolding him all the while. Miraculously, despite the swelling crowds, our things have not been stolen. Still holding him close to me, I wonder what I have turned into? A mother who hits her child, is that *me*? The girl who did not scream even once in labour; the girl who thought anger was a costly emotion; the girl who was capable, organised and unflappable backstage, behind the curtains,

25

that dancing girl — where has she disappeared? Where is the old me? When Sanju grows up he will remember me as a monster. The kill-joy whose favourite word was 'No'.

I am in a crowded, public place and I am crying openly.

A luminous moon has risen from the turbulent waters. Over on the other side, the skies are still aflame.

Will the day never end?

~

We moved to this street in 1993 from another neighbourhood south of the River Adyar in Madras, close to the beach. At that time, Thayee did not immediately make room for herself in our lives. But then, she was younger, less frail and Palani, her son used to give her a daily measure of cooked rice.

The street is L-shaped, perpendicular, then parallel to the main avenue. As one turns off the main road, one realises that the street also demarcates the area where the residential part ends and the market begins. The homes bordering the side of this market are a special element of the street; the thatched roofs, the wood-smoke, and chickens and buffaloes lend to it, at times, that primitive, tranquil air of a village. The road is narrower here and widens on the longer stretch, past the bend, where our house is located.

We are sheltered from the noise of traffic and a disturbing parade of strangers in front of our gates and, at the same time, we are close enough to the shops and the bus stop.

On this road, the cock does crow at dawn.

The area got its unofficial name from the dhobis who lived here and were prosperous once. Sometimes when I walk along its narrow, inner lanes, I remember afternoons spent hunting for ripe tamarind on the warm sand that outlined colourful shapes spread out to dry, and I can smell the boiling starch and hear the slapping sound of cloth being punished against stone. I was seven or eight then and my ayah had a special friend among the dhobis.

Thayee refuses to take herself away from this street and make her home elsewhere, to the immense irritation of Palani's wife. However, these days, it is only in the relative cool of the early mornings that she finds the strength to venture out to the main road and carry out her determined search. She is the only one of her kind here and she marks the street, in a way, by her shuffling, bare-shouldered presence. Reciprocally, the street defines her; there are spaces she can enter and spaces she cannot, the newly-built flats, for example, or more significantly, her own son's house.

~

Sanju is drawing a plane. The possibilities of a flying object fascinate him. Planets, rockets, planes, he draws them all. In his box of crayons, the single steel grey colour is his favourite.

Appa is filling his pipe. He carefully separates strands of tobacco from the pouch, pressing them into the bowl. It is a skill he taught me as a child—neither too loose, nor too tight. He observes Sanju, a look of abstraction on his face.

Then he speaks, 'You know, when Swami Vivekananda was a little boy, he liked to draw. His family would buy him water colours that cost some...four annas a box and he loved painting with them. He was very naughty as a child, probably naughtier than Sanju. So his mother complained to Shiva.

She said to him, "I asked you for a son but you sent me one of your *gana*s instead". '

Appa lights his pipe and extinguishes the match, waving it rapidly.

'You see, she prayed to Vireshwar, Shiva, for a son and she also asked a relative in Benaras to worship the deity at the temple on her behalf every single Monday, for an entire year. Bhuvaneshwari Devi herself, the great woman that she was, fasted and prayed to him in Calcutta. One day, she dreamt that Shiva would grace her by himself becoming her child. She woke up with the sensation of being covered in light. And in time, she did have the son she desired. But then, Shiva has his own way of answering prayers. Take Markandeya for instance. His parents had to choose between a brilliant son who wouldn't live long and a son of average intelligence blessed with a long life.'

'Like Shankara,' I add.

Appa laughs in agreement. 'What a child Shiva gave her! Actually, he gave Bhuvaneshwari Devi not one but three sons. Vivekananda had two younger brothers. Now *this* child, her eldest son, he was naughty and full of energy, getting into all sorts of mischief. And he had a spirited mind as well. He would tease his two elder sisters, make them run after him and then leap across the open drain where the poor girls couldn't follow. "Catch me!" he'd say. Or he would argue.'

I smile. It is a familiar situation. Appa draws on his pipe. The aroma of tobacco swirls around him. He settles deeper in his chair. 'He had been taught not to use his left hand, you know, like all of us. One day while eating, he saw that it made sense to use the left hand to pick up the tumbler of water, since the fingers of the right hand were coated with food. So he argued about that and would not listen. Threats and punishment had no effect on him. Later, he said that one should never make a child fear something.

'He was restless. How was this energy to be contained? Ultimately, after trying various methods, his mother found the only way of calming him down. She would pour cold water on his head, whispering "Shiva, Shiva" in his ear. It always worked.

'In fact, when they wanted to name the child, they asked her to choose the name. So, she looked down at her baby, his life-breath the answer to her prayers, and she must have seen something in his eyes—a spark, an immense depth—something, for she was quiet for a while, lost in thought. Then she named him Vireshwar...They all called him Biley. Narendra was the name given to him later.'

I imagine her bringing up her son, but it is difficult to picture him without the robes and the turban. A little, rounded shape in a dhoti. I see a sturdy child whose face is all cheek; plump cheeks that compel one to pinch them, pull them, love him. Thick black hair parted in the middle. Liquid mischievous eyes, of a shape divine. When he smiles, he reveals a gap, a fallen tooth. Merriment radiates from him as he climbs the forbidden champak tree or closes his eyes during a lesson. The thrill running through her when he repeats a *shloka* effortlessly, having heard it only once or when he sits on her lap and puts his arms around her and asks why Hanuman has not appeared in front of him even though he has waited for ages in the banana grove. In the next second, he is up and about, racing to his pet goat.

'There was always apprehension in the family that he might take after his grandfather and renounce the world. Once he wore a *gerua kaupina*, nothing else but that tiny piece of ochre loin-cloth, and went about the house saying, "I am Shiva. I am Shiva." Think of what she must have felt and suffered, when he did take *sannyasa*, renounced the world. There are only two people a *sannyasi* bows to. His guru, of course, and the other, his mother, for she gives him permission to take *sannyasa*.'

Appa points at the air with the curved stem of the pipe for emphasis. 'It's *she* who has to learn renunciation first.'

Bringing up a *swami*. A naughty *swamiji*: the thought engages me. Did she ever lose patience with him? Smack him on his cheek or bottom, and then regret it when he was grown, dressed in ochre?

'He was an extraordinary man. He remained deeply attached to his mother to the very end. Normally, as you know, to become a *sannyasi* is to say that one's former life has ended. That Narendranath Datta died the day Swami Vivekananda was born. But not him. He was deeply concerned about his mother. That is the living Vedanta; that was what he was all about. Nowhere does it say that Vedanta and love of one's mother do not go together or for that matter love of ice cream! Swami Vivekananda loved ice cream. Chocolate ice cream.' Appa puffs happily on his pipe. To him, Vivekananda is a presence.

After a pause he continues, 'A gentleman came looking for him once, in the hills of Almora. He knew him by the name Naren and that is the name he used while asking for him. The boy at the door of the *ashram*, must have been a *brahmachari*, the boy told him that there was no Naren Datta there. Narendranath had died a long time ago, but there was a Swami Vivekananda. He could meet *him* if he wished. Now Swami Vivekananda happened to hear this conversation and asked the boy, "What have you *done?*"

'Then he asked for the guest to be shown in and when the guest called him Swamiji, naturally, after what had just happened, Vivekananda immediately responded with, "When did I become a 'Swami' to you? I am still the same Naren. The name by which the Master used to call me is a priceless treasure. Call me by that name."'

Appa transfers the beloved Peterson pipe to his hand, and I know he is enjoying the warmth of the bowl against his palm.

'He was not one to be bound in any way,' he continues, 'least of all by notions of what it is to be a *sannyasi*. Towards the end of his life, he would say that he wanted to live in a small house by the Ganga with his mother. Look after her, do *seva*. But that was not to be. Maybe with this thought in his mind, even at a time when his own health was poor, he took her on a pilgrimage to East Bengal and Assam. This was about a year before he died. He wrote a letter to Sara Bull, his American mother, saying that he was trying to fulfil this wish of hers.'

I marvel as Appa quotes from memory. The words come alive in his rich, deep voice.

'First Vivekananda announced, "I am going to take my mother on a pilgrimage." Then he said, "This is the one great wish of a Hindu widow. I have brought only misery to my people all my life. I am trying to fulfil this one wish of hers."

Sometime after this, when his health deteriorated further—look at the problems he had, he suffered from diabetes and asthma, his one eye was damaged by a blood clot—he did not drink a single drop of water for two months as a cure. Around this time, his mother remembered a vow that she had made: as a child he had fallen very ill once, and it was so serious that his mother prayed to Ma Kali. At that time she vowed that if he became better, she would send him to the temple to get *darshan* of Ma Kali. Somehow, it escaped her mind and the vow remained unfulfilled. Worried about his health, she asked Vivekananda to help complete that promise.

'Obediently, he, the Swami, the great *Shaamiji, Maharaj,* as the Bengalis call him,' Appa lifts his hands, miming adoration, 'famous, and adored by thousands, *he* took a dip in the Adi Ganga, and even though he was sick, went the distance to the temple in wet clothes and prayed to Kali, just as his mother wanted him to. He was Swami Vivekananda but he was also her son.

'He was truly concerned about her. When he went to the World Conference there was another Bengali there, Mazoomdar from the Brahmo Samaj. Well, he saw how this young Bengali was adored by the audience, he saw that and became jealous of his success. When he came back to India, he spread beastly rumours, terrible lies, that Swami Vivekananda was immoral, that he was associating with white women. This of a man who attributed his many strengths to the power of chastity: his *brahmacharya.*

'The Swami wrote a letter—I'll find it in his collected letters and read it out to you—what he says is that it really does not matter to him what anyone should think of him. He is a *sannyasi*, a voice without a form as he once put it, but if his mother were to hear such things, it would cause her unimaginable pain.' Perhaps without even intending to, Appa has located my fear, too overwhelming to be articulated, and soothed me in an indescribable way. Naren's mother, she too had a child who was difficult to manage. She *complained,* to Shiva. But that did not diminish her love for her child. Neither did the complaint diminish her child. Look what he grew up to be!

Within me, an idea unfolds its wings; hope makes its way from her life to mine.

~

The ground beneath the neem is covered with greenish-yellow twigs, small dry leaves and pale new flowers. The flowers when brown and withered are soft and springy to tread on barefoot. Sometime during the day, Thayee will sweep them to one side, making a little pile that the breeze and passers-by will scatter again.

She hides a sheaf of coconut leaves, the bucket, the cardboard and the paint can inside the compound of the widow's house. The shabby roll of cloth, she places on top of the wall, near the gate. Her things safe, she hobbles away; the space is left bare. The overlapping ridges, the imprint of sharp broomsticks raked through sand, are like a fleeting souvenir of her presence, drawn only to be erased and created anew.

~

That divinity abiding in every being in the form of consciousness,
I bow my head before Her, again and again and again
and yet again.

That divinity abiding in every being in the form of intelligence,
I bow my head before Her, again and again and again
and yet again.

The room is dark. My left arm encircles Sanju's waist, registering his breath, his fight with the blanket, the seconds to silence. A mosquito drones annoyingly close to my ear.

He is asleep! Peace descends, finally, on the house.

I wait for a minute, just to be sure, before rolling away from him and switching on the light. Only his head is visible, the hair untidy, grown out of the cut. I tuck the sheet into the hollow below his face. He sleeps on his side, his legs curled, the way I had pulled him into the curve of my body, a soft wall of protection.

I gaze at him, absorb the colour of his skin, the eyelashes punctuating his face, the nose that is straight, delicate, so unlike my own. When he was a baby, his ears seemed huge, set at the side of a miniature face. The proportions are correct now, the other features having caught up with the ears. He is small, my baby, tender. He sleeps, gathered safe on the lap of *Ishvara*.

What a storm of energy he is when awake! Unbelievable! I bend down and kiss him softly on his cheeks, a stream of affection, a blessing surging from me. For one mad, fleeting second, I should like for him to be awake again, to look into his sparkling eyes.

34

Given back to myself, I can now love him in peace.

There is one more ritual to be completed. This particular day surpassed, I give myself an 'A plus' and five stars as a mother. Aditi, the dancer, gets an 'F' for not even trying.

While undressing, I catch sight of myself in the mirror. I stare at the reflection of the girl. *Girl? Woman?* I am not quite able to find myself there. My face is puffy with tiredness. The breasts having grown heavier, sag. Two u-shaped curves join in at the navel, delineating muscles that refuse to lie flat. Miraculously, I have no stretch marks. My thigh muscles resemble those of a weightlifter, developed over years of practice. An image of the Earth Mother from the Harappan era comes to mind: the bountiful flesh, the abundant breasts. The solid immobility of that body captured by a master artist.

I laugh aloud, wanting to cry.

Impulsively, I reach for my make-up case. When I was ten and danced for the first time on stage with seven other girls, it was the licence to wear bright red lipstick and pancake that told me I was a dancer, and not that I could dance. Over and over again, we rubbed the cheap, sticky lipstick on our lips, all the time admiring ourselves in a spotted mirror on the wall of a dusty green room.

I pick up an eyebrow pencil and start drawing around my eyes. How many times have I performed this ritual, this transformation?

Grease the pencil tip with some cream and fill in black within the outline; the quicksilver eyes of a dancer.

'You have small eyes,' my guru once told me casually. That remark stayed with me, and I examined it frequently for signs of a prediction. Did it mean I could never be a dancer because I had small eyes? Or, that I needed to work more with my eyes for they are small?

What *did* he mean?

For days after that, I was jealous of girls with big eyes and long lashes.

The difficult part now, the extension of the black kohl towards the temple, two lines encircling the eye and tapering to a point. When done properly, with symmetry, the eyes look like that of a doe-eyed goddess. Next, the eyebrows arching like a bow over those kohl-elongated eyes. A bindi in the centre of the forehead. A twirl of the pencil and a small black beauty spot appears beneath the large red circle. Lipstick to match, not the garish red of childhood but a rich maroon.

My very first costume was of yellow silk, shot through with red. It was expensive, for the silk had a heavy border of gold. Amma said that I looked like a flame on stage during my *arangetram,* the debut as a solo dancer. The blouse that matches it is tight but fits after a struggle, provides lift. I wear the costume, the hooks fitting on the first eye. I can get into it!

I cannot stop now.

I am seized by this madness. The box of jewellery is hidden beneath my saris in the cupboard. I pull it out and open it after a long time. Cabochon rubies set in gold, laced with cool white pearls. The distinctive style of temple jewellery reveals itself. I catch my breath. Each one of these pieces has a name. I recite them softly as I wear them. *Talai saman, raakhodi…*They fly to their appropriate places, along the parting of the hair, dangling beneath the ears, tight around the neck and then a flow of pearls down the chest to the pendant with a swan motif, the *padakkam.* Bangles.

I switch on the single spotlight that was specially installed for the purpose. Light pours over me. I look at the mirror and see a beautiful dancer, flowers in her long, long hair. Not as slim as the Harappan dancer—one hand cockily placed on her hip—but glowing. The only time that beauty has ever mattered to me: during every appearance on stage. Passion and intensity, given unreservedly to the love of my life: *Dance*.

There is one thing missing though. The rows of ankle bells, the *ghungroo*s. But if I were to wear them, their confident, brassy jingle would wake Sanju up. *Would he recognise me now?* I turn away from the mirror; tears do not befit that proud vision.

~

We met at his office, high above ground, sealed from the hot, humid, outside world by air conditioning, electronic locks and security cameras.

I sat in my friend Shweta's swivel chair, enjoying the chilled air, the tiny but powerful lights sparkling in the ceiling, the sense of gliding in a short, idle arc.

He passed by, stopping to place a file on her desk. Shweta was his boss.

'Aditi, this is Murthy. Murthy, Aditi.'

He handed me his card as our names met in the space between us.

'It's plastic, can't be torn.' He was visibly pleased with such an advance, the show-off in him evident even then.

'Really?' I said, tearing ineffectively at it, then frowning at the barely creased rectangle in my hand.

Leaning against the wall, arms folded over an expensive blue tie, he grinned. His upper lip disappeared under a moustache in need of trimming, the beginnings of a double chin hinting at self-indulgence. He wore suspenders over a long-sleeved shirt, a passing fashion trend that none of my friends had adopted.

Behind him was a zigzag of open cubicles. In one of them, a man typed away rapidly, staring intently at a screen.

Shweta was watching us.

I crumpled the card slowly in my fist, but it sprang back to its original shape, light, translucent. Looking all the while at him, I folded it to the last tiny bit and threw it into the dustbin. Nonplussed, he stared at the bin, a small crease appearing between his brows.

Shweta invited him out to lunch with us.

As we mixed ghee with steaming rice in the enormously satisfying *thali* at the Woodlands, he spoke of having gifted an entire year's books to a classmate in college who could not afford it.

Such a generous gesture; I wanted to be friends with him.

~

One of the mango trees in the garden is barren. The clean, tender leaves it has sprouted are like fountains of light green upon the darker, dusty basin of the old. The other tree, which is in fruit, has new leaves of a colour so indescribable, so distinctive that it takes its name from nature itself—*maanthalir*. Everyday, the squirrel makes its way, headlong, down a stem to the raw bunch. It sniffs, enquires loudly after their state of being and bounds back into the heart of the tree. Everyday, I contemplate the mangoes with jealous intent, wondering who will get them first, the squirrel or the urchins with stones.

Thayee, whenever she spies them, will screech ineffectually at the boys and chase them away. Sometimes, she will threaten them with a stone, her hand drawn back, ready to strike. Just two days ago, she scared a boy so much that he lost his balance and dashed his cycle into the wall. His mother, who works in the doctor's house on the corner, marched up to Thayee and a street fight was on.

'What did my son do to you, uhn?' was the mother's refrain.

Thayee swore that it was he who had harassed her, run over her almost, and that she had acted in self-defense.

The woman was furious. She grabbed Thayee by the arm and yanked her to her feet. Thayee swayed, her voice rose high in a scream of fear, she clung to the telephone pole for support. The woman dragged her son forward, a thin boy wearing frayed shorts, about ten or eleven years old, and held him before Thayee. 'Look at his knee!' she shouted accusingly, 'it's bleeding. Who'll pay for the doctor and the medicine and the bandage, uhn?'

Thayee continued to protest loudly; neither woman listened to the other.

It was evening.

People drifted into a semicircle, attracted by the fury and drama of it all: the next-door watchman, a toddler wearing nothing but a black hip-cord, the opposite-house driver who had arrived midway, Sanju, Poongavanam, and two strangers.

I watched from the bathroom window upstairs which had the clearest view.

The mother yelled some more and, in another fit of anger, shoved Thayee against the wall. A ripple of excitement shot through the crowd. They moved in a little closer. Sanju, who hates raised voices, saw danger to Thayee and running up to the woman pummelled her with angry fists. I barely had time to see her pause and look down at him in a blur of rage before I raced to lift him out of the commotion.

In the minute it took to reach the gate, the woman had exhausted herself. She bore her son away to their home at the market-end of the street. Thayee sat down with difficulty, muttering incoherently to herself and the crowd dispersed, half-disappointed, half-relieved that nothing more had happened.

Sanju who does not know what fear is, nor danger, dug his elbows into my chest, placed his palms firmly against my cheeks, immobilised my face and told me all about the bad woman who had been angry with Thayee. I held him tightly, very close.

Later, the woman returned with her son. He had a dazzling white bandage around his knee. She showed it to Thayee and filled with the burning sense of injury done to her child, she shouted at her again. Thayee was silent, indifferent almost. She cursed Thayee, swore at her and finally when the only action left was to be violent with her, she backed off saying that it was Thayee's age that had saved her that day. There was no way of making out who was in the right but I was glad to see the woman go.

~

The bowl is full of dal and rice mixed with extra ghee. I started feeding him twenty minutes ago. He has grudgingly accepted three spoonfuls. Something vile rises in my throat.

I feel nauseous. What if I just left it, did not feed him, waited to see if he approached the food instead. You've tried that, I remind myself. Nothing had happened. He'd just become irritable and aggressive. I don't know what else to do. I force myself to lift another spoonful.

Amma passes by.

'You should put more dal in his rice. Make it thick, that way he'll get more proteins. Why aren't you giving him vegetables?'

A nerve throbs in my head.

'What's the point? He's not interested in food. I'm sick of this!'

'You got him so easily, so soon after marriage, within six months. I don't understand why you feel this way. You have no idea of how terrible it is for women who want a child but cannot conceive. You should thank god for all that you have been given, including this wonderful, intelligent child. Look at Roshan, look at her life with Sweety. I have never heard her lose patience with him even once.'

'It's the other way. I feel I am wasting the gifts that I have been given!'

'It's only a few years more. You can dance all you want then.'

A few years in a dark tunnel that presses close upon me. I wake up each morning anticipating night, wanting to slip through the day without mishap. I have set aside days with great satisfaction, like money in the bank. Days imprisoned in the squares on the calendar, have come free, blurred, made indistinguishable. I have survived a day, and then another, a week, a month. Saturdays are the worst. This thing that impels from within, that bites, that burns, she does not know it.

'A few years later, I will be older. I might not have the same flexibility, the energy to dance!' A sense of futility washes over me, debilitating in its effect. 'Leave it, there's no point in saying any of this to you. The thing is, you never wanted to do anything with your life.'

Amma is taken aback. 'It's true,' she says.

Her degree certificate—a professional one like mine, her medals—now tarnished, lie buried in some remote corner of her cupboard.

I hold the spoon against his lips, wanting to jump out of my skin and run.

~

An old friend of my parents, Roshan Aunty, arrives in a black Ambassador. Sanju loves her; she who comes bearing gifts, she who plays hide and seek with him, giggling like an eight year old.

He tugs at her handbag even before she has seated herself, eager to see what is inside. She pulls out a comb and a mirror, pretends to admire herself, and chuckles excitedly as Sanju pulls the mirror out of her hand. He plays with it for a while and turns again to the capacious bag. *What lies in those depths?*

She pretends to search for a huge gift, dislodges the contents of her purse. Triumphantly, she holds aloft a pencil torch. Sanju is silent for the next ten minutes, unscrewing parts, trying to get at the minute bulb inside. She claps her hands, laughing gaily as he finally reaches it. '*Shabash*. Well done!'

When I emerge from the kitchen, bearing tea and snacks, she is down on all fours on the Persian carpet, a horse playing with a pony. She shakes her head menacingly and Sanju giggles. He has completely forgotten me. What a relief not to have to pay attention to him. I play with other children the way she does with him; a giddy response to an adorable creature towards whom one has no responsibility.

'Sweety is in the car. Will you give him some lemonade? He likes it the way you make it.'

When the lemonade is ready, I walk out to the car, quelling the brief spasm of terror, a remnant from childhood.

He leans against the cloth-covered rear seat of the car, his head lolling, staring blankly at the crow regarding him from the porch. I call out to him, a whisper almost. He has a big body and had seemed like a hulking giant even when I was little. The driver takes the glass from me and wraps Sweety's fingers around it. He lifts it to his mouth and in one gulp the lemonade is gone.

Inside, my parents are trying to have a conversation with Roshan Aunty despite Sanju. She slides a piece of her thumb out, feigning great pain, showing him a stump. He grabs her hand and the thumb extends, restored miraculously. She is so amused by the look on his face, she presses her nose on his, gives him a bear hug.

Sweety looms on the threshold.

He stands awkwardly, a child in a man's body. Six feet tall, wearing yellow knickers that end high above his knees. He would have been handsome had intelligence animated his eyes. His arms hang by his side, passive. Roshan Aunty is up in a flash, leading him to the bathroom, her right arm around him. She is his universe, her very touch his apprehension of it.

He shuffles back to the car, helped by the driver. Jaw slack, his head is angled up, as though he is searching his path on the sky.

I take a deep breath.

Roshan Aunty returns to her tea, now cold. There are deep lines on her face. Her lipstick is bright, hair recently styled. When she was younger she dressed with flair, a sense of fashion.

No, she does not want me to heat it up.

The terror of visiting them at their home... As a child, I would close my eyes, hide behind the chair as he was led to another room. With the terror was a nebulous sadness as well: a nameless sense of distress.

Dismayed by my fright, Amma reassured me, told me that Sweety was gentle and would not hurt anyone. Something had gone wrong when he was in Roshan Aunty's tummy and he was born with a mind that did not keep pace with his body.

Later, when I had grown up, she added that it was a failed attempt at an abortion that had led to this. The tablets Roshan Aunty had swallowed had not been strong enough to kill.

Her husband was embarrassed by Sweety, wanted him banished to an institution but she remained steadfast, turning down the suggestion each time it was made.

She is sixty-nine now, a widow and she dreads extinction. What will happen to Sweety when she is gone? Who will look after him with the same love and care? Only she understands his cryptic language, every nuance of those guttural syllables. He is thirty-one, a baby forever.

They leave.

She posts extravagant flying kisses to Sanju from the open window of the old Ambassador, waving as long as she can see him.

'Come again soon,' he shouts to her.

~

There are two guardians of the mango tree—Thayee and the opposite-house driver, otherwise enemies, but united together in this common purpose.

On weekends and during summer holidays, the boys will insist on playing at our end of the street where there is more shade. Frequently, the ball lands in Amma's garden and they embark on adventure.

The bravest among them will surreptitiously raise the latch of the gate and tiptoe in, convinced all the while that he is invisible. He will search for it, his gaze travelling not only along the ground but up across the mangoes as well. Sometimes, just when he has sighted the rounded green object half-hidden in the grass and is creeping stealthily towards it, a sari-border will appear on the periphery of his vision and he will, knowing no escape is possible, freeze, pretending to be a stone. Amma will seize the mango, chase him away and warn the others not to play in front of her garden.

Later, to his delight, Sanju will find yet another ball growing in the grass; a fruit in his Ammamma's magic garden.

The boys and Amma rehearse this thrilling scene every once in a while. Over a period of time they have learnt to deal with her. They regroup a little further away and then, inch by inch, slide back to their positions under the tantalising branches of the tree.

Slumped behind the steering wheel of the Maruti, the driver watches them lazily, and just when the game has reached an interesting point or their keen eyes have wandered sideways and up, he springs at them from the small car, roaring and clapping his hands, forcing them back, closer to their homes.

~

The gleam of sweat on his bare torso, glimpsed sideways. Murthy's back is innocent of hair. Thank God! Gold-bordered cloth thrown over a shoulder, seated next to me, he concentrated on what the priest was saying, trying to enunciate unfamiliar Sanskrit words. Soon it would be my turn to recite them.

Woken at four in the morning, pushed and pulled by enthusiastic aunts draping nine long yards of silk, propelled to the *mandapam*, I was lost in a dream-like trance.

Centred in front, the blaze of fire was held within an arrangement of bricks. *Kolam* drawn by an artistic finger around this had dried into a delicate white fortress of decoration. The wavy line passing near my feet was slightly pasty, still damp. Coconuts, turmeric, sandal, ghee, cow-dung and wood for fuel, silver platters loaded with fruit, sweets, prosperity and a folded leaf for a ladle. Surrounding us, priests, parents, relatives, excited children: participants all in this ceremony.

The fire was fed. It flared dramatically, the primary witness to this union.

A choreography seen many times earlier; now I was within it, within the space, the time in which this ceremony unfolds — my wedding.

I was crossing over, leaving girlhood behind, seated on Appa's lap. Seated precariously, feeling like a butter-ball swaddled in the customary drape of my sari, worried that we will both topple off this narrow metal chair.

At the auspicious moment — with furious drum-beating and sustained high notes on the *nadaswaram* that are both an announcement, and weapons against sounds of ill-omen, he stood before me, his hands moving past my face, and as I gazed downwards, I saw two m-shaped pendants in gold dangling in front of me, then pulled closer to my chest as the three knots were tied in the bright yellow thread, somewhere over my bent neck. Someone was rearranging the garlands, displacing their weight — brief respite.

A shower of flowers, petals and rice-grains fell on us. Some fell on the priest as well, and remained there, fine yellow petals and raw rice decorating his bare back.

Sakha saptapada bhava...

With these seven steps, let us be friends
I seek your friendship, may we never deviate
from this friendship.
May we walk together
May we resolve together
May we love each other and enhance each other
May our vows be congruent and our desires shared

This is what we asked for. This was the important, the desired — companionship.

As we walked around the low well of fire, counting steps, I could feel the heat from the sacred flame. Sweat trickled past my ear, an invisible, clammy lotion spreading beneath all the finery. He was ahead of me and I noticed stray pink flowers and turmeric-touched rice grains caught in the folds of his cotton garment.

Wedding silk, ancestral gold, a garland of tuberoses pricking my shoulder, ghee feeding a fire, an ordinary hall transformed by the magic of herb-infused smoke and busy ritual beneath a fragrant canopy of flowers and mango leaves.

Beside me, this familiar yet largely unknown man; my husband. And on my toes, silver rings glistened, finally.

~

It seems that nothing excites passion as much as the fruit of a tree. This was the root of the quarrel between Thayee and the driver.

It was one of those rare afternoons when the street was quiet. Earlier, a lone woman had come crying *'Todapey!'* in three powerful, elongated notes: half-plea, half-advertisement. She was young and carried four or five of the bundled reed-brooms on her head. She looked like a strange creature with long wavy stalks sprouting horizontally from her skull. A black four-petalled bow drooped from the very end of her thin plait. She looked up and seeing me at the window, tried to persuade me in her hoarse vendor's voice to buy one. I ran to the bathroom window and just as urgently tried to persuade her in loud whispers to go away; Sanju was fast asleep. She stood hopefully at the gate for a while and then left. There was peace after that.

Then, rough, frenzied hands hauled me abruptly out of the dark well of sleep. I lay still for a while, my arm curved around Sanju's sleeping form, trying to wish away the discordant voices, resenting them deeply, but it was no use.

Sanju stirred and woke. We rushed to the window.

The driver was in a magnificent rage. He had caught Thayee red-handed! He stormed up and down the road, addressing himself to whoever happened to be there at that moment, or he stood in front of Thayee and shouted at her, the pointed tip of his beard bristling with every spasm of emotion that overcame him.

Thayee was holding on her own against the lanky, grey-haired, volatile man who was probably as old as her. It was impossible to figure out what she was saying—quite often she wears out her opponents by screeching in that indistinct, mumbling way, so I concentrated on the driver.

'Must have been early in the morning, when no one was there, and no one would have known but for me,' he proclaimed loudly and theatrically for the benefit of the day watchman. At this point, Thayee must have said something particularly offensive, for he strode up to her and said, 'Shut up or I'll—' He gestured a warning with his hand. The heavy metal strap of his wristwatch flashed in the sun. Thayee was unfazed. She continued to protest, 'Give them back, they're mine, mine,' slipping in an abuse here and there.

The watchman was happy for the diversion that had broken the long tedium of the afternoon. He sat on a stool placed outside the ornate gate of the new flats and listened attentively to the driver. I could see him clearly because the tapering top of the ashoka tree had just been cut then.

Thayee and the day watchman were like two points marking the two extremes of a line; the driver rushed from one to the other like a shuttle flying across the loom.

'How come she had so many of them, tell me…?'

'The old woman hired a boy, that's how…'

'Be quiet, shut up you wretch!'

She was getting to him because at times he would raise his voice even more and become very agitated, and I feared he would harm her for sheer provocation. I was still no closer to knowing what it was all about.

Fatima's mother appeared at the gate, head slightly bent, her palm shielding her eyes from the glare of the sun. Wisps of hair had escaped from the bun she usually wears, making her look younger, vulnerable somehow. She looked pained at having to deal with Thayee and the driver in the middle of the afternoon.

Eagerly, the driver began telling her about Thayee and her loot. He spoke in a version of Urdu that is perhaps best described as Tamilian and I had to make the larger collage with a few word-pictures snipped from his impassioned, tangled narrative: coconuts, boy, thirty-one, early in the morning, hoard, discovered, stolen, there in the vacant house. As final proof, he pointed upwards to the tender coconuts visible on the tree growing at the very edge of their compound, near the wall.

Thayee did not present her case.

Fatima's mother was not entirely convinced by his story; no, he was forced to admit he had not actually seen them doing it. She ordered him to return Thayee's things to her and when he continued to yell at Thayee in an attempt to save face, she said, very quietly but firmly, 'Ab bas, chup, quiet now.'

The driver, sulking bitterly, brought mature, unhusked coconuts by the armful from just inside the verandah and threw them on the ground beside Thayee where they lay like a collection of discoloured, battered soccer balls. He made several trips from his gate to the one next door where Thayee, crowned in wet, dirty rags, sat like a queen receiving gifts from a disdainful, elderly courtier.

There remain though questions for which I haven't found answers: How did Thayee get a boy to pluck all those coconuts without making a sound, from right next to the watchman? Were they the fruit of some other distant tree or was it the watchman who...? And, why did the driver go looking among her things anyway?

Whatever the truth might have been, from that day on, Thayee and the driver stopped speaking to each other.

~

'Maa, what does die mean?'

'It means one stops breathing.' *Where did he learn this word?*

'Will I die also?' My heart skids.

'Some day, when you are very, very, very old.'

'What does *it* mean?'

'Remember I told you that *Bhagavaan* or *Ishvara*, God, is everywhere? The part of god inside you is called *atman*. When you die the *atman* goes back to *Bhagavaan.*'

'And then?'

'It becomes a baby again. With a different name.'

He is silent, working the idea.

I enfold him, contain all his limbs within me, inhale the essence of his being.

May it be that my years are added to his.

~

Appa calls out to me. Sanju is shelling peas with Amma. He is quiet, engrossed.

An oasis of peace in the stormy desert of waking hours.

'Here it is. I found Swami Vivekananda's letter. Aditi. Listen to this. Written on April 26, 1894. He was in New York then. A pamphlet has been published about him in Calcutta, full of praise, with extracts from different newspapers and he says:

> *Now I do not care what they even of my own people say about me—except for one thing. I have an old mother. She has suffered much all her life and in the midst of all she could bear to give me up for the service of God and man; but to have given up the most beloved of her children—her hope—to live a beastly immoral life in a distant country, as Mazoomdar was telling in Calcutta, would have simply killed her.*

'It is in the letters that one finds an approach to Vivekananda. One knows him best through his letters.

'There is this other letter that I simply must read to you. It must have pleased his mother, of course, but greater than that must have been Vivekananda's own happiness in his mother's joy. Wait, let me find it.'

He bends over the book. His hair is all silver, I realise with a shock. Swept off his wide brow, fine, silky, it curves over his collar. He needs a haircut.

'Aah. Here it is. Listen!

> *Dear Madame,*
>
> *At this Christmas tide when the gift of Mary's son to the world is celebrated and rejoiced over with us, it would seem the*

time of remembrance. We, who have your son in our midst, send you greeting.

His generous service to men, women and children in our midst was laid at your feet by him the other day, in an address he gave us on the ideals of 'Motherhood in India.' The worship of his mother will be to all who heard him an inspiration and uplift.

Accept, dear Madame, our grateful recognition of your life and work in and through your son.

And may it be accepted by you as a slight token of remembrance, to serve in its use as a tangible reminder that the world is coming to its true inheritance from God of Brotherhood and Humanity.

With great regard

It is signed by twelve women, Sara Bull and eleven others on the Christmas of 1894. It would have given her great joy, don't you think?'

He lapses into silence, both of us travelling to a home in a narrow lane in Calcutta where a mother is sought out by an excited relative.

There is a letter from America in *her* name. She is in the kitchen. She wipes her wet hands on the edge of her sari and hurries out to receive the rectangular piece of paper.

Everyone in the house gathers around her as she opens it.

'Look at the circumstances of his family at the time he chose to renounce the world. It could not have been easy, as the eldest son, to tell Bhuvaneshwari Devi, now a widow, that he was leaving home, that in the days to come he would perform the death ceremony of Narendranath Datta, her Biley. He describes it so well. He says that when he renounced the world, from one side of the eye there was a tear of sorrow for his mother and from the other, a tear of joy for the glory of the ideal he was about to embrace.'

Appa is wearing a new veshti. It has a plain maroon border with a line of gold running through it. The starch makes it stiff, stand away from his calves.

'It is a paradox really that a *sannyasi* can help anybody in the world but not favour his family because he has left that life behind in becoming one. Vivekananda did not forget his mother. On the contrary. He wrote to the Maharaja of Khetri in 1898.

'Aditi, listen!

'*After trying these two years a different climate, I am getting worse every day and now almost at death's door. I appeal to your Highness's work, generosity and friendship. I have one great sin rankling always in my breast, and that is to do a service to the world, I have sadly neglected my mother. Again, since my second brother has gone away, she has become awfully worn-out with grief. Now my last desire is to make Seva and serve my mother, for some years at least. I want to live with my mother and get my younger brother married to prevent extinction of the family. This will certainly smoothen my last days as well as those of my mother. She lives now in a hovel. I want to build a little, decent home for her and make some provision for the youngest, as there is very little hope of his being a good earning man. Is it too much for a royal descendent of Ramchandra to do for one he loves and calls his friend? I do not know whom else to appeal to.*

'The Raja of course replied immediately. So eight days later the Swami wrote to thank him and he said:

'One thing more will I beg of you — if possible the 100 Rs.
a month for my mother be made permanent, so that even after
my death it may regularly reach her. Or even if your Highness
ever gets reasons to stop your love and kindness for me, my
poor mother may be provided [for], remembering the love you
once had for a poor Sadhu.'

Appa closes the book, moved to tears.

I take it from his lap, wanting to look again at the
photograph of Bhuvaneshwari Devi. She sits cross-legged,
prayer beads in hand, looking straight ahead. At the time of
record, she is a widow, unadorned. She wears white and a
dark shawl is thrown over her sari. Her back is straight,
manner regal, and her beautiful eyes are inward looking.

~

No one knows exactly what it was that led to Palani
throwing Thayee out of their house.

Some say he had forbidden her from going near the
rubbish heaps. It was a matter of honour; people were
laughing at him, his mother lowering herself to such a level!
He first threatened to throw her out if she continued this way
and then one day he actually did so. Some say it was his
wife who made him do it; the details have been forgotten, the
fact remains.

Strangely, none of the people I question seem to have
much sympathy for Thayee.

~

We will be too tired, we had agreed beforehand, feeling
very grown-up in discussing *it*. We would wait past the 'first'

night to explore this aspect of married life. I was relieved. Late-night parties, close dancing, weekend trips out of town with other couples, through it all he had never pushed to go beyond the occasional hug, a kiss on the cheek. Such strength of restraint, a man prepared to wait, is a sure sign of his innate decency. After all, he has to be as eager as me to know what it is like. He'd never had a girlfriend, but implied in a vague way that he was experienced, that there was a brief fling with an older woman.

And so, there we were, the first night in his home, in the room he had helped decorate with flowers. We could finally be seen entering a room together and closing the door behind us! There was the awareness of his parents elsewhere in the house, of the ribald amusement of others.

Regretting the brief while in which I got to wear all my jewellery, saved, hoarded, bought, for this day, I removed them slowly, savouring their beauty: this, my grandmother's necklace, this, Amma's diamond ring. The light over the dressing table was dim. I had to peer into the mirror to look at myself—*was I looking nice at the reception?* The beautician had piled my hair into a complicated arrangement, studded with pearls. Searching for pearl-tipped hairpins buried in my hair, I made a stack of those already discovered.

Our garlands hung by the door. The heady perfume of deep pink roses spilt into the room, made of it a bridal chamber.

Dressed in a cotton nightie—lots of pretty lace on the sleeves and the front—assailed by a healthy, apprehensive curiosity, I turned towards him. Glad to be married, glad it was not to a stranger, glad to have negotiated the overlapping worlds of tradition and modernity so easily: within caste, to one's choice.

He switched off the lights. A strip of plastic glowed orange in the dark, the mosquito repellent. Swiftly, he moved to the bed, leaving me no choice but to join him, feeling a little odd. Warm his hand, gentle his face against mine, agreeable those new shifting sensations. Held in his arms, made secure, soon, a button hidden within lace was undone, then another. His silk *jibba* had been unceremoniously tugged off.

The shock of it; to be completely naked in front of another person. Neon vapour, entering the dark room from the streetlight outside, evaporated mid air. Nothing was visible though and the garment of night hid him, also naked, from me. *What does it, glimpsed in passing between the legs of naked street-urchins, look like?*

Instantly, his body was over mine, the press of bone and muscle; rough hair against my cheek. Breeze stirred by the creaking fan touched me where the blanket shape of his body did not impede it. Something distinct becoming close to my thigh, bumping into a crease of skin. Entry sought. His hand moved downward, blatant in its urgency to position. Delicious, this moist sliding pressure, this soft-sheathed firmness. At the threshold of being; beyond — a glimmer of unknown pleasures.

An agitated spasm and then he was still; breathing hard, he dipped his head onto my shoulder.

This is it? All that fuss about this?

Through that dark cloud of incomprehension, a rainbow of relief; it did not hurt. Somewhere in the distance, there was the piercing whistle and tap of a roving watchman and I became aware of my puzzled dismay, a path scraped raw inside me. Drawing my legs together, I turned towards him to ask, but he was asleep.

Did he like my nightie?

Uncomfortable mattress, hard cotton pillow, an unsettling stolidity about this home of durable cement and windows dressed in iron-mesh. Rectangular silhouettes of gifts piled high on a table promised excitement on the morrow, dispelled obscure dread.

A bus trundled by on the main road outside and transmitted its vibration to the wall. Slowly, the sounds of traffic ceased.

~

That divinity abiding in every being in the form of sleep,
I bow my head before Her, again and again and again
and yet again.

That divinity abiding in every being in the form of hunger,
I bow my head before Her, again and again and again
and yet again.

Thayee refers to it as though it happened just a month ago, but a year or more has passed since that day.

I turned the corner and was halfway down the road, when I noticed people standing around a body. I knew from the hair, uncombed, like a crown of tarnished silver, that it was her. The car swallowed the entire distance. I drew up to one side and saw the rest of her: calloused palms open to the sky, the small length of her inert body, the worn piece of cloth barely adequate in the dignity it offered. The cord that she had wound tight so many times released itself, dread spinning in me like a leaden top.

I had to park at a distance, and as I walked back, I noticed that the people around her were our new neighbours, two houses to the left. We had not met until then. Mother, father and son.

She lay on unclaimed territory, the strip between their wall and the tarred edge of the road, beneath her, the roughness of untended grass, gravel and small twigs. She moaned, her eyes opening only to collapse shut against the painful dazzle of the sun. Something burst, like a tiny bubble, inside me.

Alive!

Relieved, grateful even, to find community of concern, I addressed the semicircle, 'What happened?'

The son answered, 'She's got high fever. She's too weak. My mother gave her some buttermilk, but even that she has vomited out. I have made her swallow some medicines. It should be taking effect. I have given her some tablets yesterday also, but she did not have them.'

There was something in the way he said 'I'.

'You're a doctor?'

He nodded, 'She's having fever since yesterday.'

So we did not have to take her anywhere immediately. I turned my head away from the doctor to stare down the road at a hut with mud walls fronted by a small pen. Part of the road, at the bend where the two arms of the 'L' met and formed an angle, had been fenced off with bamboo stakes to form a pen. There was just enough space for the two cows tethered there to stand side by side as they swished their tails at the flies. I expected a figure to emerge any moment from the hut and come running towards us, but was disappointed.

'Her son?' I could feel the top of my head burn, sweat bead a transparent moustache over my lips.

He shook his head. 'We sent a message. He is not there, it seems. The daughter-in-law refused to come.'

'But someone has to look after her…'

He nodded in agreement, 'What to do?' Then he shrugged and said, 'But if he refuses to look after his mother, there's nothing we can do about it.'

We debated in silence, caught in the quicksand of indecision. It is a complex business, this fluid, invisible accounting of debts owed and favours granted: how is one to know the exact measure of action by which a karma is ended or a fresh one initiated? How does one balance an insubstantial but eternally accurate scale? Debts coming to fruition, how much had fallen due to Thayee?

Every now and then her body trembled. She was wandering far from us, in the fevered plains of her mind. Sweat glistened on her brow, like a trail of slime on black soil. Then horror exploded the fragile barrier of hesitation: I saw a line of red ants crawling along the narrow seam of shade where her left arm met the ground.

'She has to be moved. We can't just leave her in the sun.'

Further down the road was a group of labourers, lounging on a heap of river-sand, pretending disinterest but looking in our direction furtively. Their relaxed air, suggestive of sloth and a great lethargy, was deceptive. In a few minutes, the afternoon shift would begin and they would return to work. Two of the men were persuaded to lift Thayee.

One held her by the armpits, the other gripped an ankle in each hand, and together they carried her, her frail body swinging on a hammock of warm air, to the other side of the road, to her habitual place under the neem.

The doctor's mother offered an old bedspread that was folded into four. The men lowered Thayee on the narrow pallet of cloth and returned to the construction site. She rolled on to her side, knees and arms folded within the curve of her spine.

I shook open a bedspread that I had snatched off the clothes-line and it billowed gently before assuming the shape of her shrunken body—a comma embossed on its smooth, clean surface.

We stood on the bright road for what seemed like a long while, black, crumpled shadows circling our feet as though our darker, indifferent selves had peeled off incompletely, holding us there, stuck fast.

Her son had abandoned her entirely to the care of strangers. He did not come, that day, or the next.

~

When I teach Sanju that the divine is everywhere, immanent in everything, what does that really mean? I am teaching him about the ideal, but am I living it? What would it mean to live within that thought, one's consciousness totally immersed in it?

Appa is delighted. 'Aaah. To ask this question *is* to take a step forward on that path. You see Aditi, while the luminous and powerful philosophy of Vedanta tells us that there is no difference between "them" and "us", for we are all part of the one Reality that pervades the entire world, very rarely do we *live* that ideal fully with a conscious understanding of what it implies. Those who do, having achieved inner realisation, are considered the best, and the most elevated in Indian society; saints, great souls. Read the Upanishads, read Vivekananda, discover yourself. Start with his letters.'

Behind him is the beloved wall of books — tall, plump, dapper, squat — light resting bright within letters shaped in gilt, glazing the orange spine of a paperback.

'Sixth shelf, fourth column from the left. There, next to that big red book, the Gospel of Sri Ramakrishna.' I locate the books on Appa's bookshelf, run my hand along their spines, their colours known, familiar within the mosaic of myriad book covers.

~

The sun shines adamantly outside. A red butterfly twinkles past. I stare out of the window, dreaming. I shall write about becoming a mother, describe motherland. When all five of my fingers opened, and a flower bloomed, bee-like lips drank the honey of a maiden's blossoming face. A thumb extended slowly from a fist and the jerky motion of that adorable Balagopal, Baby Krishna, was captured, placing his big toe in his mouth. Once, my fingers played on Krishna's flute and forest animals stopped in their tracks... entranced. Now they shall dance wistfully over a page, holding a pen.

At the heart of all movement there is a great stillness.

Where do I begin?

A smile tugs at my lips. That moment was so long ago, I have almost forgotten what it was like. Since then, I, avid collector of tips from magazines, have had no one to practise with. Just last week, I read an intriguing one involving peppermint.

What shall I name him?

Naresh? Srini? No, Pradeep.

From the sphere of the moon, a movement to space. From space to air. From air, a descent in the form of rain. From the joyous fall of water, a journey to the centre of a plant, a grain of food.

The man is the fire. His mouth, open, its fuel, his life breath, its smoke. Speech, flames. The eyes, glowing coals. The ears, sparks. Into this fire, the gods make an offering of food. From that, arises semen.

The woman is the fire. Her inner hidden part, fuel. The hair on it, a cover of smoke. The opening, a burning flame. Entry inside, coal. The sensations of delight, sparks. Into this fire, the gods make an offering of semen. From that libation arises a human being.

This from the *Brihadaranyaka Upanishad*.

The sheets are cold against the length of her body. Moonlight slants through the window, coming to rest across her feet and the floor like a white quilt that has half-slipped off the bed. In the otherwise dark room, the mirror on the wall becomes a painting in water, holds a shard of light immobile on its tenebrous surface.

We make choices in loneliness that we would never make otherwise, she muses as he crosses the room, a silhouette dipping in and out of a stream of silver. He sits beside her, removes his watch. Cloth freed from the propriety of buttons, a languid complicity.

An absurd affection surging within her at the touch of naked skin, she hugs him close. The brief, agreeable sensations, of a feather of warm breath on her temple, a moist flicker roving into her ear, are a rudimentary, suspended journey into the fabulous domain of the senses.

Loneliness has a different meaning now. It is to hear his breath quicken, feel his fingers play uncontrollably with her hair, his concentration turn inwards, away from her, until all senses converge. He lifts himself away, eyes closed, exhausted, 'Thank you, Thanks. That was great.'

Missing the tumescent warmth weighing into her, she turns on her side to observe him. Remote, she looks at him with curiosity but he is in a blissful haze, oblivious.

'Pradeep?'

'Hmm.'

'What does it feel like?'

'Great!'

'Describe it...'

'Hmm, it's...I don't know how to...You have to feel it to know. It's...great!'

She knows how his body responds to her, she steers it. It is a game now, to see how soon, how many times, in what way. The disdainful slide of her hand, the deliberate suck of her mouth or within her.

Retribution for leaving her behind; for not making the effort to carry her with him.

He travels distances, reaches wondrous places, before sliding into a tranquil sea. He has left her behind, a shell washed onto a dry sandy shore, abandoned by receding waves. It is a solitary place from where she can hear the sound of the ocean, see the height of the exhilarating waves that bear him aloft, from where she can only guess at the depth of the waters that wash over him.

Inside her, thousands of wriggling entities charge speedily to a round mass waiting for them. Of them, a single one is successful in piercing the outer mantle. A subtle body, sukshma sharira, *like a caterpillar, has negotiated its way from the end of one leaf of grass, one life, to the beginning of another. It has known her before, cherished her many lifetimes over, in different relationships.*

Impelled by thought, drawn by desires, carrying a portion of the entire granary of its sanchita karma, *the subtle body animates the fused entity.*

Within her, a city, brahma-pura, *of human form is being shaped for it. Food forms its first wrapping.* Prana, *breath, enters the womb, reaffirms the great wonder of birth, the mystery of rebirth. She, innocent, disappointed, is unaware of it, yet.*

~

It is a picnic everyday. Sanju is seated on the bonnet of the car. We watch the world go by as I hold the next spoonful to his mouth. 'See the butterfly, there, pretty, no? Say *aah.*' His tongue pushes against the food, allowing very little in. I had begun feeding him an hour ago. My legs ache. The bowl is half-empty, but it is also half-full. I want to grasp his head with one hand and thrust the food in; down his throat ...The violence of the image scares me. A sparrow hops nervously on the gate, anticipating a banquet.

The water lorry arrives, breathing smoke and roaring mightily. I make capital of the flurry. People converge on the blue tanker, bearing narrow-necked pots like babies on their hips. Some carry buckets. There is a rush to fill water from two outlets that are generous for four minutes. There are shouts of irritation, of tension. The taps are then shut and the driver moves, leaving behind a disarray of containers and puddles in the potholes on the road.

Liquid sloshes in tubs and pots, buckets and drums whose dull plastic colours brighten in the sun. Women in pairs swing the bucket like a toddler between them; they walk to the rhythm of its weight. The street is now a waterworks: a giant filling station.

'Take a big bite. *Eat!*' His attention is everywhere but on the food.

The first mango of the season. I feed him a scoop of heaven and hold my breath. He likes the pulp, rejects the fibre. I persevere, though inside I am crumbling.

Four times a day, seven days a week, time is measured in meals.

If he grew up never to read, or without manners, would it matter? But if he does not eat, he will not grow. Underfed, he gets cranky. That is the rock and the hard place. I am caught.

Words reverberate in my head, mocking at me. *A city,* brahma-pura, *of human shape is formed for the* sukshma sharira...*Food forms its first wrapping.*

~

A secret hidden in the *Garbha Upanishad.*

Within the womb, the new body is complete with all the features in the ninth month. The being obtains memory. It remembers its past birth. Deeds done, deeds left undone. It remembers the nature of karma, the good, the bad, intentional, unintentional, the consequences of its actions.

It broods, speaks to itself.

Many different wombs have I seen. Thousands. I have eaten different kinds of foods and suckled at many different breasts. I have lived and died and taken birth again, again and again. I have done things for the sake of others, in their interests. While they enjoy the fruits of those efforts, I am accountable for my deeds.

Filled with anguish, it frowns, somersaults, frantically kicks its tiny feet.

'*What is to be done?*'

It makes a solemn resolve.

67

*If I can escape from this womb, take birth as a human being,
I will seek refuge in that which destroys misery and grants freedom
from the distressing cycle of births and deaths.*

I will take refuge in Sankhya Yoga,

Or,

Maheshwara.

Or,

Narayana.

It enters the birth passage, an instrument almost, expanding, contracting, and is propelled out, squeezed, pressed upon, in great discomfort.

Touched by life, it forgets.

~

Live in the moment I tell myself these days, try, but there are some moments and their aftermath that I have lived through too often. Sanju skips ahead of me, trying to get to the car first but he trips and falls.

I am far from him but from the way he stands when a man passing by picks him up, his right leg buckling, jelly-like, under the weight, I know it was not a simple fall. Nothing seems to be broken though he cries a great deal and is in pain. The entire night, like Babur, I ask for his pain to be transferred to me, but my prayers are not answered. In the morning, I tell him we are going to the hospital instead of school.

'Bone doctor?' he asks.

We wait for forty minutes before it is our turn. The air inside the waiting room is tired and dense. It lies coiled around us as though it has snaked its way through every room in the building, gradually acquiring the weight of sickness, and is too exhausted and germ-ridden to move.

Sanju remembers the doctor from the time he broke his toe and is happy to meet his friend again. He addresses him by his name, which amuses the doctor greatly. He has no fear of a strange place. Everything is an adventure, even in pain.

An x-ray establishes that there is not even a hairline fracture. There is, however, an accumulation of fluid in the area around the knee. He is to rest and not run around. There is a big orange torch on the doctor's desk. While Dr. Mani and I discuss the prescription, he dismembers the torch. The doctor does not find that amusing.

It is sad to see Sanju walking instead of speeding. He cannot run even if he wants to. It takes something like this to make him slow and careful.

I spend the entire morning in the hospital.

~

Murthy calls. He has got a promotion. His title is long and sounds very impressive. This is the most excited I have ever heard him sound.

It is a strange paradox. I, who treasure solitude, have found myself alone in a marriage and very alone in bringing up my child. It wrings from me the kind of strength that I do not want to possess.

A man who has no love for his child; such a person exists. It is a discovery made hesitatingly, with disbelief.

The baby shows great consideration to him in choosing a weekend to enter life. When the staff at the nursing home demand extra baksheesh because he has had a boy, Murthy looks stricken. He does not take a single day off from work after the birth. He mutters something about losing sleep when the baby cries at night and moves permanently to another bedroom. His son is not even a week old when he wants to register him in a boarding school.

I remember the night when Sanju had a fever that crested flimsy hurdles of medicine, and kept surging like a tidal wave upon him. I sponged his little body, holding him close until dawn, trying to soothe him. I worried about the drops of medicine lost, dribbling out of his toothless mouth, weighed the decision to give another dose over and over again while Murthy slept downstairs, unconcerned.

I celebrate this changing, growing human being all by myself. The third month passes, then the sixth, and the first birthday. My child has survived my inexperience, my mistakes: the time I wanted to give him a nice hot bath and nearly boiled him alive.

Another memory.

Sanju is now three years old. He is jumping up and down on the divan. He misjudges distance and falls against the window sill, in front of our startled eyes. When I pull him away from the cement edge, I find a gash on the right side of his head. He is writhing in pain. Murthy laughs at me when I say that we must rush him to the doctor.

'It's nothing. They will not even waste a bandage on it,' he says casually.

Lata holds Sanju in her lap while I drive to the hospital. One of my first visits there in emergency. The wound needs to be stitched; his hair is shaved around the tear.

When I give Sanju a very short haircut, the scar is visible.

Murthy works out restrictions imposed on him in his childhood, withholds Sanju's toys, gives them to him grudgingly, insists that pieces of toys be counted and put back. The same poison has entered me. I find myself sometimes auditing pieces of puzzles or coloured pegs when I collect Sanju's toys. Nine out of ten, one missing, a thorn stuck in the mind.

I recount the latest of Sanju's accidents.

'Get him one of those space suits, nicely padded, with a big helmet. Better still, why don't you stay in the hospital itself? That way you won't have to rush there.

'What do you *do* the whole day long?' he says before disconnecting. 'You are just wasting your time.'

He makes being selfish seem so attractive.

~

A friend from school, Ramya, has organised a reunion. Three classmates have converged in Madras for the summer. Our children play together, running round and round the well in the backyard of her home, their voices pitched high in excitement; it seems incredible, like wealth pooled high on a platter.

This well, like others in the city, has run dry and a screen has been placed over its circular mouth for safety. It stands there like a reminder of another age, the pulley rusty from disuse.

I relinquish charge of the children to a maid and return to where my friends are. I stand on the verandah, about to enter inside when I see them, rapt, held within a moment, an iridescent bubble that I hesitate to rupture.

'Mine has a lingam on it,' says Priya, peering down at the *taali* that dangles on the heavy gold chain she has pulled out

71

from beneath her kurta. Her baby is six months old, a boy. She is rocking him to sleep on her lap.

'You don't wear corals? Look at these, such huge ones. I didn't want but they insisted at my wedding,' says Sangeeta, who teaches in a school. We share a common predicament, of once having been independent, earning an income, of wanting to make something of our lives but finding it more difficult than we had imagined.

The four of them, like the children we were at school have placed their *taali*s on the palms of their hands, and they pull closer into a huddle on the Pattamadai mat, knees resting against the other's thigh or foot, looking at the minor variations in all the jewellery strung upon heavy chains of gold. *Why does mine, beneath my sari* pallu, *feel so light?*

'Don't tell anyone,' whispers Sandhya, her eyes widening. 'I can't sleep with it on, it pokes me. So I put it under the pillow. One day I almost forgot to put it on in the morning. *Abbaaa!*'

They chuckle as she hits her chest in mock relief and the *taali* disappears from view once more, kept safe from eyes that might harbour bad intent. A scientist, she is away the entire day and the old in-laws are put to work parenting her two children.

Whenever I meet Sandhya's daughter, a plump, lovely little girl, her hair gathered in two ponytails, I see an unspoken, barely articulated question lurking in her eyes. She is eager for the affection I give her, pulling her cheeks, stroking her hair.

It is given to us, our individual expression of what it is to be a mother. Leaving Sanju in a crèche or sending him to school in a van with an unproven driver, are choices I reject. My parents tire after playing with him for a while. The television is not to snare his attention. One negotiates time for oneself within such a construct.

There is only one girl in my dance class, who continued with her career after her child was born. She left him with her mother, weaned him by the time he was three months old. The child grew up thinking the grandmother was *his* mother.

I step over the threshold, moving towards the group of young women. It is an old house in Mylapore. The room has a high ceiling with beams running in parallel lines across it. It is cool here, for the walls are thick and the solid pane-less wooden windows kept shut. In this space, time seems to be held at bay, recalled only when it comes to lighting oil-lamps and performing *Sandhya*. The stone floor is burnished with red oxide and there is hardly any furniture, just a table against the wall.

'I think the kids are hungry.' They look up even as they settle the folds of clothing over their *taali*s.

'Come, come, let's start! It's all ready, I've made maangaa-saadam from our house mangoes,' says Ramya. She was the school head girl. Intelligent, outgoing, everyone thought she would make a career for herself. She has three girls and is simply happy bringing them up.

Priya is the last to get up. Her baby is wide awake, perched on her arm, head bobbing unsteadily.

I reach out, hands clothing his chest and he sails through air into my arms.

Light, so light, I have forgotten the feel of a baby, its head against my cheek, warmth radiating through soft bone, fine hair. The baby tries to climb me, its small feet pressing into my stomach, my chest, gurgling all the while.

My friends gather around me, attentive to the baby peering over my shoulder, talking to it, admiring its dimpled fists, its perfect feet, trying to entice it away. It clings to me, refuses to be impressed by their flattery.

'He likes me!' I say triumphantly.

'So, now you live with your parents?' asks Priya.

I nod.

'It was a rented house,' I explain.

'Your in-laws?'

'They live with his brother in England.' I can read the speculation in her mind.

'How's Aasha? You must be missing her. You two would always be stuck to each other in school.'

'She's in Columbus now. Two kids. She's not very happy out there.'

Priya's eyes glaze. It is a question rarely asked of others: 'Are you happy?'

'Have you given up dancing?'

The question stings. 'No! I'm just waiting till he goes full-time to school. I practise when I can. How to explain... he's accident-prone. The minute he comes back from school, I have to watch him, follow him everywhere so that he does not hurt himself. I don't have a maid either.'

'I wanted to learn Bharatanatyam when I was a kid. My father would not let me. You learnt from such a famous guru, Tanjavur Santhanam! Such luck! You were so good, how can you give it up for that long?'

'My guru is sixty and he still performs. Actually, that is the miracle of classical dance. The older one gets, the better one's *bhava*, emotions expressed with the face. I mean, hopefully it gets better with age…with some famous dancers, it is the other way around! They are past their prime but will not quit.'

Sanju sees me holding the baby and is upset. He runs over to me, will not stop tugging at the edge of my sari *pallu* until I hand the baby back to Priya.

'Jealous!' she chuckles, watching as Sanju jumps up and is swung onto my hip.

Laughing at the pleased look on his face, we walk towards the backyard to collect the children. It is a one-to-one mapping, each of us a specialist in our own child; what she likes to eat, where he gets tickled, the manner in which they approach sleep. It is our children who have taught us this, given us our narrow but potent expertise. We are now, indisputably, aunties.

~

The moon is hidden from sight. A street lamp flickers madly accompanied by a buzzing sound. I rest my forehead against the window grill, staring at the garden below, drawing strength from the solidity of the trees, their presence living and real within the shadows of the night. The tears start, but the sobs are muted for closeby sleeps my child, his hands bunched under his chin.

I have come upon a great secret hidden in the open, it seems. All those mothers with babies, idealised up until the time I became one myself, were all bravely fighting tiredness and anxiety and low spirits. I think of photographs taken of me, with Sanju in my arms—Madonna and child. When I look at myself in the photograph, I see tenderness and love on the smiling face that is automatic in its response to the camera, but what the negative does not capture is the inside, the frazzled nerves, the melancholy and fatigue.

I carry the weight of my dreams. Yet, seen through other eyes they appear flimsy, inconsequential, light as air.

My parents brought me up as me, not less for being a girl, not more for being intelligent. The 'I' that was, fashioned assiduously by parents, teachers and me over twenty-five years, stopped being, disappeared in an instant.

It is a paradox. A dancer in the classical idiom, I was taught to transcend the body. In forgetting the body, the awareness of self, through *bhava*, one comes closer to finding the truth, that one Reality. After years of thinking that the world was mine to conquer, this role that emphasises my female body comes as a shock.

What do I do with my mind while I feed him and bathe him and tend to him, with love, with care, with my entire heart?

Those very qualities that brought me success as a dancer — dedication, mad fearless courage, imagination, single-minded concentration — *am I to fold them neatly, put them away until required? Is it possible to disassemble oneself in this fashion?*

It is tiring to cry. I have no energy left. I put my arms around my younger self, the girl before whom all doors were open, but she is not consoled. *Why was I born? Why was I born? What was I meant for?*

The moon slips out of a cloud and the mango leaves on the nearest branch are visible, like blank faces turned towards to me.

I must sleep now. I have to wake up early, take Sanju to school.

~

It is the first day of school, after the summer vacations. Six thirty in the morning. I stuff pieces of bread and butter in

76

his mouth. 'Swallow,' I plead, as I guide his hand through the sleeve of his T-shirt. 'Swallow.' Forty-five minutes later, he gulps his milk and we race to the car. I escort Sanju to his class and he shoots, without a backward glance or even a kiss, to where his friends are.

A tap on my hip; an invitation to play.

I turn around and see Joey, Sanju's best friend. It is time for our game. I must try and catch him. If I succeed, I can plant a kiss on his cheek. Most days, he lets me win. He wheels all over the playground now, taunting me, calling me by a name special to me, 'kissing-girl, kissing-girl'. I love it. I grab a handful of shirt and claim my prize; the feel of fresh cheek rounded by a smile.

The bell rings and they skip into line.

I shall go and see my guru, practise dance—I plan as I leave the gates of the school. I have earned this reprieve; three-and-a-half hours in which to live my life.

When I reach home, I see his toys lying under the chair, the carpet humped in odd places and begin to pick them up. I rearrange his clothes in the drawer, iron his uniform for school, put toys back on a shelf, treat myself to fresh bed sheets and when next I catch a glimpse of the clock, it is time to reclaim him.

~

Suddenly, we carry company in our heads. The day I discover them in my hair, I make Sanju sit on the floor in front of me and part his hair, searching. Oddly, he likes the idea of looking for them and sits still, bending his head this way and that as I scan his scalp. He must have got them from a friend.

I find an engorged adult and show it to him before squashing it between my thumb nails. There is a most satisfying burst. I put a live one on the palm of his hand and he is fascinated.

'So when the lice dies, it becomes an *atman*?'

'Er, yes.'

'And then it is born again as?'

I decide never to kill one again, except by medication.

~

'I fell in school. Blood came.' Sanju mentions it casually. He is examining a battery, wondering how to open it.

'You fell? How?'

'Playing. I got okay but.'

I examine his clothes. There is no blood on them. There is no bandage, nothing that hints at injury. Sometimes he embroiders fact.

'Where did it hurt?'

He pats the back of his head.

'Does it hurt now?'

He shakes his head. I relax.

The next hour passes with ease. He is hungry and actually opens his mouth for the next bite before I ask. If only every meal were like this, I think, if only. He has a long conversation with Ramya Aunty on the phone, is absorbed in a puzzle, and then is sleepy. I lift him up onto my shoulder and am putting him to bed when I feel him scratch his head. Did a single louse escape the treatment? I sit him down, grab a comb, draw it strongly through the back of his head and see blood. I die.

There is a circular wound the width of a pencil. The crust came off with the comb. A thick drop of blood trickles down the nape of his neck. I rush him to the hospital. They shave his hair and close the wound with a single stitch.

When he sleeps at night, the bandage is like a four-petalled white flower at the base of his skull. In his five years of life he has cut a lip, broken a toe, worn the cast out thrice, suffered from chicken pox, had two stitches at the side of his head, and now this.

I brought a perfect baby into this world and am dismayed to find his smooth, unbroken skin bearing scars already.

~

It is that time of the morning when the road is busy with vehicles, when children leave for school and the office desk is yet a journey away.

The koel that lives in the neighbour's garden sings loud piercing notes like a series of questions, 'Koo-u? koo-u?' The bird, unseen, exists in the purity of its voice, the direction and distance from which it emerges at familiar hours of the day. There, ahead of me, within the medicinal cool of the huge neem tree.

Over the shriek of birdcall and the rapid chatter of squirrels, two voices make themselves heard. Amma's, pitched high, aggravated beyond endurance, and Thayee's, low, persistent. The voices move, traversing the path that leads to the front of the house.

'No, no, NO! Absolutely not!' She switches to Tamil, 'Look at the mess you made the last time. I don't want to see a single thing of yours here. No. Take it elsewhere. C'mon, quick, pick it up. If you don't, I will.'

'It's just one small bag. They steal my things. They stole my money, just a few days ago. I'll keep it here for some days only.'

'It's not one bag, but two. You think I'm blind or what?' Amma breaks off abruptly, vexed by the argument. 'I'll go mad with this woman, really! There's a limit to everything. *Seekram, seekram,* quick! Take it out or I'll...'

From behind the curtain, I peer down at the garden. If Amma sees me, she will appoint me translator, wanting me to convey the exact shade of her anger, irritation and exasperation to Thayee and since my tone will not match hers in pitch and expression, inevitably I will be the recipient of that which is meant for Thayee.

So, protected by the curtain, I watch.

Below me, Amma emerges on the driveway, her head a black pollen pad amidst the yellow nightgown flowing about her. She marches out of the gate, lugging a polyurethane sack, the sort in which cement is packed. It has been tied with a piece of brown jute string; the slack at the open end drawn tight into a narrow frill of plastic. The sack bulges in three places in a shape that is unmistakable. She disappears beyond the green screen of mango leaves. Thayee follows slowly, still arguing.

Poongavanam who was sprinkling fistfuls of water on a small area in front of the gate pauses in her work, straightens herself. There is a self-conscious, slightly embarrassed look on her face as though she is not quite sure with whom her sympathies should lie. She wipes her hands on her *pallu* as she watches, frank in her enjoyment of this unexpected interlude. Where she stands, the ground is damp, dark, like an oil stain on the dusty brown fabric of the road.

Amma returns and waits for Thayee to leave. She has not heard what Thayee was saying all along,

'Let the bag remain. They will steal it, my only other sari, I have nowhere else to keep it. Let it remain here only.'

In her voice there is neither apology nor appeal. It is the unmindful, almost firm voice of someone impervious to disgrace, someone who has already fallen quite low.

Amma has to struggle with the latch before it clangs shut on the gate. She has forgotten about the bag.

Outside, Thayee settles the white, misshapen sack like a child on her hip and hauls herself into the compound of the house across the road. Legs set wide apart, Poongavanam bends from the waist again. She holds a coconut half-shell in her left hand, her fingers stretched like prongs around its rough, fibrous exterior. Taking a pinch of rice powder from it, she drops a row of white dots on the slate of dampened earth, her movements now slow, preoccupied.

The morning, which seemed to have choked on the tiny sharp bone of disquiet, starts to breathe easily once more.

~

'Why does one have a child? For *this*?'

Amma is irked by the question.

'A child is a joy, in your old age he will look after you.'

Who knows when death will approach? The child might not be there, at that point in time. Does one create a human being to have a nurse for old age? My mind shrinks from the idea.

The thought of Bhuvaneshwari Devi comes to me. She died in 1911, nine years *after* her son.

'There is no point in just saying these things. One must feel them. Joy, joy, where's the joy? I am too tired at the end of the day to enjoy him, play with him. There are days when he must think he has a shrieking banshee for a mother or a zombie—No. NO! Do not do this, don't touch that.'

I sigh.

'It's a stage. It will pass. Then you will say that he is not spending any time with you. You troubled me as well. I used to feed you milk spoon by spoon. All the neighbours used to laugh. I had Farex in my hair most of the time. I changed my sari thrice a day, after every meal.'

It is a story I loved hearing when I was a child, narrated in tones of mock exasperation and great love.

'When I was having you, I worried every minute. What if you did not breathe, how was I to teach you breathing? What if there was no milk to greet you with? When you were born, the first thing I did was count all your fingers and toes. You talk as though you are the only mother in the world to have discovered the effort involved.'

She continues, 'Sanju is a delight, so responsive to everything around him. In fact, one of the attributes of a *paramahamsa*, Swan of Enlightenment, is that he is like a five-year-old child.'

I am up against a wall.

She and I, mother and child, are not the same as Sanju and I. She had a *girl*. I got a whirlwind. Besides, I was a quiet child, happy to observe the world and locate myself within it. Sanju engages with the world in a different way, he wants to break it open with a hammer.

The *paramahamsa* barges in and the conversation halts. I say: he is an immensely tiring child to bring up, but my words

82

are translated as: I shall abandon him. *Is it such a great betrayal of motherhood, to complain? To speak of things as they are?*

Her legacy of love, I do want to pass on to him; only it is being dented, battered out of shape.

~

White hair, white garment, a body parched brown by the sun; she lies immobile beneath the parijatak which does not offer her much shade, left arm tucked under her head, the right arm resting along the curve of her side. The octagonal flagstones beneath her are hot. The sun is at its peak. Every time I see her like this, a thin cord of dread winds itself around my heart.

Scared almost, I walk cautiously towards her. 'Thayee? Thayee!' She could be dead, she could be alive. But I am too soft, 'Thayee!' I have to scream. Her eyes open; bewildered, they search for the sound of my voice.

'I've got to take out the car. I'm late.'

She struggles to get up, lifting first her torso then her hips, palms pressed against the concrete. She rocks for a while on her haunches, knees locked, before shifting her weight to her legs. Minute particles of sand pattern the dark skin on her forearm, some of them rolling off as she moves. I hold her just above the elbow; her skin is surprisingly soft and fleshy.

She walks slowly towards the gate, insisting on opening it for me.

'Why don't you sleep on the *thinnai?* Then you won't be in the way and it's cooler there.' She looks at me blankly and I give up. It isn't worth the effort to shout; sweat is sliding past my ears, already.

As I reverse the car out of the driveway, she says, 'Why must you go out now, in this boiling heat?' At times, homeless old woman that she might be, it is hard to subdue one's irritation.

~

A coconut hurtles towards the ground; the sound falls like a rock into the still waters of the night. In the morning, I look for it on the thick spread of grass and under the crotons and lily plants bordering the lawn. It is gone.

~

That divinity abiding in every being in the form of reflection,
I bow my head before Her, again and again and again
and yet again.

That divinity abiding in every being in the form of energy,
I bow my head before Her, again and again and again
and yet again.

A great bolt of lightning escapes from Indra, rends the sky into two jagged parts, and speedily returns to him. I wake up with a start. The rains have arrived. It is a celebration, water bedding with earth in the stillness of the night. The breeze is chilly against my bare arms. I check to see if Sanju is properly covered. The skies are lighter than the shadows, a dark, smoky blue. I see a great moving wall of sound, the wind rushing into spaces and the raindrops, points of light caught on the tips of leaves.

Water collects everywhere; in the flowerpots, on the sunshades, in the buckets used for the garbage, on the roads. Already, the driveway is flooded. It slopes towards the gate and the area near the road is submerged.

Something stirs beyond the hedge. I can't see what it is. On the periphery of vision, approaching the gate, a grey polythene sheet bobs up and down, floating like a ghost. It affords hardly any protection against the rain, but two determined fists clutch at the ends, holding it above her head.

Thayee is awake, searching for shelter. She opens the latch of the gate and pauses, realising perhaps that the inner grills are locked. There is the narrow *thinnai* in the front, a place for her to rest awhile, but the rain is at a slant and the needle-sharp drops will find her there as well. The many hands of the wind try to push the gate open. It remains ajar, poised at strange, disturbing angles. She stands in a pool of water.

What is it that prevents me from running down and flinging open the doors to her and offering shelter from this powerful downpour? What would happen if the storeroom at the back were made available to her, just while the rains lasted? She would make a mess of it, and might never leave. I know the answer already. Why is it easier though to accept the fact that she is wet and destitute, than overcome the resistance to break barriers? A heaviness descends upon my heart and enfolds it.

Soaked to the bone, she wades slowly towards where her son lives.

~

The bell has rung. The teacher is at the door of the classroom matching pairs of opposites, tall with short, handing a child over to its parent or minder. I advance to the front and the teacher asks me, 'Is he very naughty at home?'

'*Very*. Is he naughty in school as well?' I am regretting the question even as I ask.

Sanju disappears while we are talking only to emerge at the top of the slide, visible behind her. He runs down the slope. This is possible? Half my attention is with the teacher, the other half is on him. My heart is racing. The minute his foot touches ground, the teacher's face swims back into focus.

'He is the naughtiest boy in the class. I have to hold his hands together and tell him that I'll tie them, before he will listen. He will not sit in one place.' I am not imagining my troubles then.

I handcuff Sanju and march to the gate before he can hurt himself again. He rotates his wrist inside my hand, trying to escape.

For the rest of the evening, I am in a long, dark tunnel with no light pointing the way out.

The hours that he is at school, I lay down the burden of worry, switch off the high alert on his physical safety. 'There is nothing I can do while he is at school,' I tell myself. It is a false but necessary sense of security.

~

The driver sits inside the navy blue Maruti, the steering wheel close to his chest, his head aslant, resting against the half-raised window. His white skullcap lies on the dashboard, collapsed in a soft heap. The landscape of the sky is distorted on the windscreen, the light mirrored strangely, the leaves fat and bloated.

It is mid-afternoon, the longest hour of the day, and the body slides into languor, succumbing to the stay of food within, the warm air pressing upon the eyelids.

Earlier, he had anchored the moving vehicle in a narrow fringe of shade, freeing himself swiftly to open the door for Fatima's mother. Doors slammed, some instructions were given to him, the gate opposite ours clanged open and a group of women disappeared into the dark coolness that lay beyond the verandah. Possession wholly with him once again, the driver collected his tiffin-box from the space at the side of his seat and a bottle of water. He ate his lunch with the watchman, sitting on a small square of cloth spread on the ground, right near the gate of the neighbouring flats.

Lunch over, the watchman assumed the stool again and the driver squatted beside him, smoking a beedi.

A short distance away from them, Thayee slept under the neem.

The handkerchief that protects his workday clothes when seated cross-legged, the way he lifts his trousers at the knee, pinching the crease in a deliberate manner, before folding his legs in this posture that keeps the rest of the body above the ground, these are subtleties that distinguish him from Thayee.

Flicking the spent beedi into a bush, he then moved to the car, preferring its sultry confines to the sporadic breeze outside.

Between shifts, he wears the car like an extension of his body. There being no other place that can offer comfort when he must be idle, he owns that space and makes of it a shelter, a place of work, a kingdom that travels.

He sits there now, depleting his energy. Waiting.

~

'We are all One, part of the immense consciousness that pervades the world.'

I don't wholly understand what Appa says. Thayee's and mine, our lives disparate in every way, one in essence? My eyes tell me a different story. I see a stubborn, feisty woman sitting beneath a tree, part of the distressing, visible yet ignored part of India that lives on so little and I, diamonds in my ears, float on the privileges given to me. She and I — *one*?

If it were true, how could I have ignored her every time I saw her clamber atop the stinking rubbish in a garbage container? What made it possible for me to register that sight and drive by, instead of feeling deeply pained by it? If it is true, then am I not also lying under that neem tree, fanning myself, registering that experience upon my larger Soul? Thayee and the driver? Closer in circumstance, but vastly different in other aspects, are they one in essence? What does that mean? Thayee, the driver, this wonderful mango tree, the squirrel with an upright tail, one — all one? I cannot see it. Their shapes are too certain, too concrete for that. How am I to blur these solid outlines, these distinct realities?

To be able to understand the one Reality in its complete dimension, my mind will have to stretch greatly, transform itself. Already, having returned home, it is as though I see everything through an altered lens, still beloved, still familiar, yet changed somehow.

One afternoon, I come across this passage and find a beginning, meet Vivekananda:

> *One day, the Master told Narendra many things indicating the oneness of Jiva and Brahman according to the non-dual philosophy. Narendra heard those words, undoubtedly with attention, but could not comprehend them, and went to Hazra at the end of the Master's talk. Smoking and discussing those things again with Hazra, he said, "Can it ever be possible that the water-pot is God, the cup is God, whatever we see and all of us are God?" Hazra also joined Narendra in ridiculing the idea and both of them burst into laughter. The Master was till then in the state of partial consciousness. Hearing Narendra laugh, he came out of his room like a boy with his cloth in his armpit and, coming to them smiling, said affectionately, "What are you talking about?" He then touched Narendra and went into ecstasy.*

Narendra said to us afterwards, "There was a complete revolution in the state of my mind in a moment at the wonderful touch of the Master. I was aghast to see actually that there was nothing in the whole universe except God. But I remained silent in spite of seeing it, wondering how long that state would last. But that inebriation did not at all diminish that day. I returned home; it was all the same there. It seemed to me that all that I saw was He. I sat for my meal when I saw that all – food, plate, the one who was serving as well as I myself – were nothing but He. I took a mouthful or two and sat quiet. My mother's affectionate words, – "Why do you sit quiet; why don't you eat?" – brought me to consciousness and I began eating again. Thus I had that experience at the time of eating or drinking, sitting or lying, going to college or taking a stroll. I was always overwhelmed with a sort of indescribable intoxication. When I walked along the streets and saw a carriage coming along before me, I did not feel inclined, as at other times, to move away lest it should collide with me. For, I thought, 'I am also that and nothing but that.'"

It is his initial scepticism and the honesty with which it has been recorded that draw one into following Narendra on his journey, from a naughty child to a fiery swami to the boy waiting, his things bundled, for the Great Deliverer, Shiva, to carry his boat to the other shore.

~

A mother, her son, a crocodile and a river. To this day, learned scholars debate the true nature of the crocodile.

Was it a drama staged by the boy to achieve his end? Was it a metaphor for the world of endless desires, their gratification? Did the gods help the boy out by sending the crocodile there? Some say that a celestial being, a gandharva, *had been turned into a crocodile by a curse. Relief from the curse could be obtained only by playing a part in the boy's life.*

He hears his name uttered by a soft voice, a voice whose song wafted him to sleep every night as a child. None of his disciples gathered around him can hear it, it is spoken to his heart, comes from a great distance. There is longing and affection in its tone, but there is also something that alerts him. How feeble the voice has become! He had made a promise. The time has come. He travels with the speed of mind to the southern tip of the land, materialises inside his home, surprising his frail, aged mother mid-thought.

Aryaamba lovingly brushes his cheek with her fingers, admiring his manly voice, the way his body has filled out, grown. She tries to count how many years have passed and finding it tiring, gives up. He must be eighteen, she thinks. He wears ochre; the colour suits him. Her eyes cling to him. She looks up at him the way an artist might look at her creation, something proceeded from her and yet distinct, with an identity of its own. A faint wrinkle appears on her forehead when she looks at his shaven head.

If she were to have written the story of his life, she would have written it differently. She would have married him to a good girl, blessed them with lots of children and would have kept that abundance safe around her, drawing sustenance from it every day. Instead, she had to release him into the void of the unknown.

He was only eight years old, her Shankara. The River Purna now flowed just by their house, having altered course at his request, as a convenience for her so that she would not have to walk miles to bathe in it. She heard him cry out for her and ran, ran like a crazed woman to the water. He was sinking. Something had caught him by the leg; she could not see what it was. There was nobody around to help. There were dangerous currents in the river, water spirits that pulled people under. She did not know how to swim that deep. She ran hither, thither on the bank, wringing her hands.

He kept calling out to her. Said it was a crocodile pulling him by the leg. He was in great pain. Her heart was bursting with fright. She could see a massive body gliding in the dark water, thrashing its powerful tail. He called out to her again; asked her to give him permission to take *aapat sannyasa* since he was going to die anyway. She did not know what she was thinking, saying. She prayed to Shiva—*Do what you will*. Again he cried out, told her that he was sure to die; at least this way, by taking *sannyasa*, he might get an extension of life.

Did he have her consent, her blessings? In that state of extreme distress, she said 'Yes'.

Firm of resolve in heart, mind, and body, even as he was being pulled deeper and deeper into the river, he uttered those difficult words of renunciation:

'*Samnyasto'ham*.

'*Samnyasto'ham*.

'*Samnyasto'ham*.'

Immediately, he was free. The huge crocodile swam away, never to trouble anyone else again. He waded out of the water, unharmed, smiling. The child had just got what he wanted. Adept in all branches of Vedic learning, master of them by the age of seven, he wanted to roam free as a *sannyasi*.

What would happen to her? She was alone, widowed and the mother of this brilliant, worthy son who had renounced the world. Who would perform her last rites? She looked down at him, her little son. He had not even grown past her shoulder-level, and yet he was so determined, so definite. Eight years old. A charming mix of the vulnerable and the certain.

Shankara allayed her fears, said she had only to think of him and he would be there for her.

'Promise?'

'Promise.'

He would ask their relatives and neighbours to care for her. His inheritance would be given to the next in line, so they would gladly look after her. Who would look after him, she asked anxiously. How would she eat knowing he was living on *madhukari,* food he would gather from various sources as a bee obtains pollen for honey?

Any woman who fed him would be a mother to him, was his answer. Any man who taught him, a father and his students would be his children. He made unknown realms outside their land seem a home away from this home, a welcome assured wherever he went.

She looked at his upturned, eager face and could not resist caressing it, his cheeks smooth, rounded against her palms. How could she give this up, the feel of his tender limbs, the rich glow in his eyes? Her insides were being twisted, churned. She followed him to the very ends of the village, holding her tears for later. There, he paused before a temple he had renovated and placed her in the care of Sri Krishna.

In the years that followed there was time to speak to Shiva, ask him to explain himself.

'For many, many years I did not have a child. Women in the village whispered that I was barren. My husband and I prayed to You at the great temple of Vadakkunatha at Vrishachala for many days. Then, You graced us with Your presence in a dream,' she reminds him, 'gave us the boon of a son. Said that You Yourself would be born to us. When You asked my husband to choose between sons who would be unexceptional, live long and one son who would be extraordinarily distinguished but live for a short time, he chose a son who would make us proud. I too, aligned with his wishes, asked for the same thing.

'After a while, I had Shankara. He was a plump baby. People rejoiced at all the auspicious marks on his little body. Strange things happened as he was growing. The time he was missing and when eight villagers searching for him found eight Shankaras in different places. When his father finally found him in the Vishnu temple, those eight other boys vanished. The time Mother herself fed him from her breast to stop his crying. Then the time gold poured from the heavens on that poor woman's house, the one over there. When those wondrous incidents took place, the villagers were convinced that he was indeed You.

'You never told me that You would take him away from me so soon after he returned from the *gurukula*. I was so happy this past year, my Shankara was back with me. You never told me that I would have to spend the last years of my life alone, while he was still alive. I did not say anything to You when You made me a widow. I accepted it as Your will. But now, I have to ask. Is this fair? Have You been just?'

Shiva smiled, remained silent.

News slowly spread to the village of Kaladi. Travellers, wandering sages, *sannyasis*, all brought news of a great philosopher, a boy genius named Shankara. He was in the north, her child. Was it very cold there, she worried, he always neglected himself so. What if he needed warm clothes? She tied coins of high denominations carefully in a cloth, placed it in a small drawstring purse, and sent it with a Namboodiri boy Agnisharman, who had studied with him in the village, for Shankara.

She was close to the end now. She knew. She thought of him and he was there in front of her. The joy of it!

He tells her that one day, while bathing in the waters of the Alakananda, he found a beautiful image of Vishnu. He used the considerable money she sent him to build a temple for Badri-Narayana, in the mountains far north, arranged for his classmate Agnisharman to offer daily worship there.

She is delighted.

She reclines on her bed, asks him to talk to her, prepare her mind for the journey ahead.

Shankara carries the great civilisation of the land in his head. A library, a repository of the most profound thinking on truth, the nature of this world, the wonder of life, birth and death, his own works included! What is there that he cannot tell her?

Used to giving discourses to his disciples, he begins to talk about the nature of *maya*, illusion, how it is like a veil covering the true nature of the universe. Brahman alone is true. The One becomes differentiated into the many, given name and form. In essence, it is so simple, he has described Reality in just seven words:

Brahma satyam jagan mithya
Jivo brahmaiva naparah

Brahman alone is the reality, the phenomenal world
is illusory.
The embodied soul is indeed the Brahman Itself
and is not different from It.

The thought excites him. There is so much to tell her, so much.

She interrupts him mid-flow. His words do not appeal to her. She asks him to tell her something more interesting, something she can visualise.

He thinks that describing Brahman with attributes might help, perhaps. He speaks of the glory of Shiva. Recites the many names that describe him. He of the third eye; He who holds fire and a small drum in his hands; He whose throat is stained blue with poison. She begins to see ash-smeared ugly dwarfs, ghosts, demons, cadaverous attendants of Shiva crowding into the room, and is frightened. The room seems dark, gloomy. She does not want to leave with them.

Whom should he describe then?

'Vishnu.'

He praises Vishnu, recites his own hymns, poetry. She has not heard it before. She smiles at the images she likes: Govinda crawling into the pen meant for cows, the dust raised by the hooves of the cows, coating his blue body, his play with the *gopis*, the way he stole their clothes, that naughty Krishna, and climbed up a tree. A little boy dancing on the hood of a venomous snake.

Bliss.

Supreme Bliss.

Gradually, a host of resplendent beings, wearing ornaments of gold, beautifully dressed in silks, become visible to her. They are kind, courteous, fill the room with brightness. Gently, they take her hands in theirs...gently, they draw her away.

Shankara sees a limp garment on the mat in front of him, white-haired, wrinkled, cast-off and yet a garment that had been a home to him for nine long months, had given him one of the three essentials obtained by divine grace alone, *manushyatvam*, humanity. He looks at her hand, the veins blue against the fairness of skin, remembers the way she registered his fevers by touch. As a child he would play with her gold bangles, trying to slide them up and down her entire arm, but would get frustrated by the elbow.

She, devout, sincere, had undertaken fasts, prayed continuously, avoided certain foods, eaten certain others during pregnancy so as to deliver him safe and healthy. He is aware that as the eldest, only son, *rnachyuta*, his duty would have been to repay the debts of his ancestors had he not taken *sannyasa*, and yet, when he looks at that lifeless body that he hugged as a child, loved, he knows that he cannot repay his debt to her, for life, for love.

He calls his relatives, caste-members, to come and help him cremate his mother, perform the last rites. They object on a matter of procedure. He is a *sannyasi*. He is forbidden from making ritual offerings to fire. How can he cremate his mother? They refuse to help him, bar him from using the cremation grounds in the village. They will not give him wood or fire.

It was a promise made under certain circumstances. He was yet to leave the village, live the life he wanted to.

His mother's permission was vital. He did not want her to feel he had abandoned her. His circumstances were changed now, yes he was a *sannyasi*, but he would not break his promise. Truth and chastity were paramount in achieving realisation.

With a grim determination born of anger, he appraises the big garden surrounding his house. There are not enough trees for wood. Where might he build a pyre? He looks into the distance, past the well. There is a shady grove of bananas towards the back there. He gathers some dried leaves from the ground, barks too. Inside the house, there is fibre from the banana tree that Aryaamba dried to make wicks for oil-lamps. He makes a little heap of his collection.

The smooth, cool banana stems are full of moisture. There is no wood, only leaf-sheath. They are edible, hide nourishment inside, not fuel. He razes all of them to the ground, chops off the leafy tops, is left with a mound of white, slender logs.

He rubs his right shoulder, concentrates his mind on sacred syllables and there is fire glowing in his hand. He lights the layer of dried leaves, then touching the pile of logs below, one by one, sets fire to that rectangle of moist, unsuitable material.

How will he carry her there? He tears the beloved garment to pieces, offers them one by one, an arm, a sleeve, a leg unto the fire. Breathing deeply, he stands there, watches the hungry blaze.

His relatives and the members of the community have roused something that had slept in him all the while. They have underestimated him, forgotten his true nature. With all the power of his third eye, he curses them. They will cremate their dead in their backyards, the way he had to. Learning will never come to them of a certain branch of the Vedas and no *sannyasi* will visit the village of Kaladi.

The curse held true until recently when a Shankaracharya of the Sringeri Mutt relieved the Namboodiri community of those curses. In Kerala, the River Purna, known after Aryaamba as Ambanadi, flows on.

~

I mix the last of the sambar with the rice, leftovers from lunch and set off in search of Thayee.

She has moved from under the neem to a house that is the last on our street. The house, single-storeyed, rectangular, with a flat roof, is in disrepair and has passed from owner to owner as an investment, never a home. Briefly, it was used as an office but one day, locks were placed on the doors and the men never came back.

The land surrounding the house lies fallow, but in front, two coconut trees and a big, shady tree conceal its defiant nakedness. The ground beneath those trees is bald and uneven, its surface so hard that it has checked the advancement of weeds.

When the rains set in, Thayee occupied the shallow steps leading to the front door, under the sunshade.

To make Thayee an offering of lunch is not an easy thing. There is no knowing where she would be at any point of time, and one bears the food uncertainly, looking over garden walls and iron gates, wondering whether she has already eaten.

I head for the vacant property first and find her crouched against the discoloured wall. It had rained all night. The tapering patches on the whitewash, made wet by the rainwater, give the impression of a black viscous liquid oozing steadily from over the parapet of the roof.

The sky is opaque, grey and even though it is afternoon, there is a quality of the morning in the cool air.

'Thayee!'

She cannot hear me and I am hesitant to trespass into the compound. I shout at the top of my voice and tell myself that I am not embarrassed, but she continues sorting scraps of paper. The day watchman from the flats, seated directly behind me, decides to help. He barks her name, giving it a harsh, contemptuous sound that travels across the road and over the compound wall. She hears his voice and looks up, her eyes trawling space before they connect with mine. When she smiles, her lower lip, pendulous and glistening, is like that of an elephant's.

Her stock lies dispersed all over the yard: talcum powder tins, blister wrapping, a mountain of flattened cardboard boxes, glass bottles of various sizes—some without caps and string. When the office was functioning, the men had employed Thayee to sweep every day the path leading from the rusty gate to the door, only that much space as was essential to have clean. They left suddenly without paying Thayee for her work and now it seems as though she has stitched for the land abandoned to her care, a motley garment of litter.

She empties some old rice that has hardened into lumps onto a makeshift plate, an unclean plastic wrap, before coming forward to accept the food. Standing by the gate, I transfer it, handful by handful, to the dented vessel while she invokes a stream of blessings, 'May your son prosper! May he grow big and strong! May he live long!'

Two baby crows flutter to the ground, beaks agape, the pink of their mouths rich against the glossy black. A cat bounds down the narrow, open staircase at the side of the house that leads to the roof. Thayee dines in company. She will never begin a meal without throwing a few morsels at them.

A gift of food to Thayee bestows on one the added *punya*, merit, of feeding the birds and animals as well.

~

Sanju has been fed and is to be put to bed. I am faced with a dam that is leaking in various places; no sooner is one leak plugged than another has sprung somewhere else. He sees Amma and decides he wants to play in her room. He scoots to her room and refuses to come out. She wants to make a phone call and says, 'Take him out of my room.'

Sanju thinks this is a great game and refuses to leave. My mind wilts. I have waited the whole day for this point in the day when I will shepherd him into bed. The end of patience: this is it.

'Aditi, take him out now! I have to call before eight thirty.'

He rolls over the floor, making weird noises, trying to assess the range of his voice.

'Take him out, quick, take him out!'

He runs all over the room refusing to cooperate. I catch hold of his hand and pull him out.

'Close the door, lock it,' I tell Amma.

One hole plugged, but I have a screaming, tearful child sprawled on the floor, who wants to go to his Ammamma's room.

'She does not want you in her room now. That's why you can't go in there.'

The door opens.

The dam has burst. Now Sanju will go back into the room. I give up and walk away. There is a shrill, persistent ring. I pick up the phone and am caught in a polite conversation while my nerves stretch backwards into the other room. *What is he doing now?*

A minute later, I find that Amma has played with him, put him in a good mood and he is amenable to sleep. It is now half an hour past the time I take him to bed. It will take me another forty-five minutes to actually make him sleep, so I will have my dinner at ten.

He is tranquil.

I have finished my dinner, put the day to rest and now can come back to myself. I change into my nightclothes when I hear a knock on the door.

It is Amma.

'You shouldn't have said "She *does not want you* in her room." I don't want him to feel unwanted.'

The day has not ended.

'Why can't you make him leave your room? Why involve me? I hate having to chase him to make him come out. It makes me feel like hitting him or something. I wasn't really choosing my words with care. I'm *tired*.'

I have been carrying this weight continuously, not being able to put it down and not knowing if ever there will be a time when I shall be able to put it down, if only for a little while.

'You ought to be grateful to God that you have such a bright child. Let me tell you something, if you had not had a child by now, you would have been depressed about *that*. Children are a joy.'

'Why are you are so dismissive, Ma? Isn't it obvious that I love my child? I could dump him in a boarding school or neglect him. Instead, I do everything for him! What is so bad about saying I am tired?'

What I really want to ask her remains unsaid. *Why is it that I get to hear this when, of the two parents, I am the one involved, day in day out, without any idea of when the pressure will ease? Why not call Murthy and give him the lecture?*

Surely, to give up the space of dreams is to hurt oneself in a central way? I have spent the entire waking day waiting for night as a woman might yearn for her lover; waiting to come back to myself, to lose myself in thought, to write. I wanted to explore what Devaki must have felt like, losing seven of her children before Krishna was born to her. Or maybe, think about the lines of a poem, *Karaaravindena paadaaravindam…lotus hand, clutching a lotus foot, fixing it in his lotus mouth, he lies in the concave space of a banyan leaf, manasa smarami, I call to mind that baby Mukunda*…find ways to interpret it in *abhinaya,* work on expressing emotions through my eyes alone.

That flower has been plucked and stamped upon.

We live each day. We die each day. I collapse hoping he will not wake during the night.

~

That divinity abiding in every being in the form of thirst,
I bow my head before Her, again and again and again
and yet again.

That divinity abiding in every being in the form of forgiveness,
I bow my head before Her, again and again and again
and yet again.

Day has come into being, slowly, the seven horses stretching their sleepy muscles, bearing the fiery god across great spaces vacated by the fleeing creatures of the night.

A thin, unsmiling man walks unhurriedly down the street, a wide aluminium basin wedged between his hip and a skeletal arm. His clothes, a plain shirt and a lungi, have taken on the colour of mud. He has never grown a beard but his sallow, pitted cheeks are always unshaven. His hair is rough and brown — what it looks like when left dry, unoiled. He has been awake since four, and has spent the last hour of darkness under the narrow, fluorescent lozenge of a street lamp, squatting outside the booth in the company of other men and women, waiting for the truck. When the truck arrived, he was part of the crowd surging forward to meet it, hands outstretched, voice boisterous, excited.

Cards punched, packets collected, basin filled, the men and women fanned out, like the first rays of dawn, across their separate, individual domains.

He walks with his eyes on the road, his head bent. Every now and then he will pause at a gate, unlatch it, and move sure-footedly to a place within; the window sill, the steps at the entrance or the bag tied to the gatepost. There he will leave a number of plastic packets, his basin getting lighter and lighter. On his way out, invariably, he will forget to close the gate.

An old woman reaches inside a blue bucket for a vessel. Her joints are stiff, she would much rather just sit there awhile, but she is hungry and it is time for coffee and bread. Recently, she has made herself a walking stick from the centre of a coconut frond that came crashing down on the road, inches away from her. She struggles with the stick, trying to harness her energy, locate it in the right muscles that will lift her off the ground.

The man walks past her. He has an air of abstraction around him, almost as though he moves within the capsule of his thought. He does not acknowledge her; she, intent on making her ageing body respond, does not lift her eyes to him.

The moment is dramatic but that is a secret shared by only a few. To the uninitiated, they are two people on a road, strangers perhaps. To others, a mother and her ignoble son; between them a bond – of blood, of history, of actions and their enduring consequences.

Palani enters our gate.

'You're late.'

Startled at seeing me outside, he replies, 'There was a hole, I had to get another.' He deposits the last of his load in the bag tied to the gate and the basin slides off his hip. He holds it sideways now, fingertips hooked under the rim. Drops of milk trickle from it.

On his way out, he replaces the latch with exaggerated care.

The packets lie inside the bag like two small pillows freshly cased in white. I pull them out, hating the slippery feel, the wetness and the stale smell on their surface. The morning has begun, with this minor unpleasantness and a game: I try to hold my breath until I reach the kitchen.

~

There is the grating, tinny sound of metal being pushed across the floor and a battered stainless steel vessel appears on the threshold.

Thayee.

'Oh God,' moans Amma, 'just when I finished making mine.' She reaches for the decoction.

Thayee lowers herself to the ground slowly, with some difficulty, her bare, attenuated ear lobes swinging gently. Crouching near the back door, she peers into the kitchen. Finding the wait a bit too long perhaps, she moves in the same posture, crab-like, towards the bucket placed just inside, near the wall, and rummages deftly through the mess: the wet mound of tea-leaves; limp mango skins; the empty plastic sachets; the broken bottle; the…

'What do you want?' yells Amma. 'I told you I'll give you all the milk packets, and anyway, you look through the rubbish before the man comes, so why must you do it *now*?' Her voice has acquired the jagged overtone it does when she is irritated. Morning is not a good time for her.

She lowers the flame, clamps shut the curved tongs onto the hot vessel and using it as a sort of handle, she moves to the door. Even though she bends to pour the liquid, it falls some distance, a thin fragrant stream that rises in a milky froth in Thayee's dish.

'Here, here's the coffee, do you want some bread?'

106

'Aaanh?'

'Bread! *Bread, venama?*'

'Aaanh?' she asks, face upturned at an angle to Amma. Her eyes are rheumy, unfocussed, her cheeks wrinkled further by a smile. In the cool, fresh sunlight, her hair shines silver.

'Bread, I said do you want *bread*.'

'*Kadhe sevade'mma…*' she announces somewhat redundantly, 'can't hear anything, and can't see anything since the day he hit me. One is enough. I'm not able to eat much.'

She receives the two white squares in her cupped palms and folds them in, raising her joined hands to Amma. Later, when she has finished dipping the bread in the coffee and sucking on it, when she has swilled the last sugary drop from the vessel, her hands climb up the iron symmetry of the door's grill, curve by flattened curve, as she lifts herself up. She clings to the grill for a while, almost surprised to find herself standing, and then the sound of her rubber slippers being dragged across the cemented backyard recedes gradually from awareness.

~

The wind sheds heat rapidly, turns cool. A squirrel bounds across a bridge of leaves. The light becomes softer, less bright. Polka dots appear on the road and race up my jeans. Then the deluge begins and everything is wet.

There is a peculiar bouquet of scents released by the rain: the smell of parched earth mingling with moisture, of the dried concentrate of urine and dung coating the road turning solvent again, of heat given off by the road, and of ripe neem seeds, of grass and the flowers of the champak tree ahead.

Sanju jumps on a trampoline of joy.

'Rain bath! Rain bath!' says he, naughtiness glittering in his eyes. Heavenly intervention has extended his playtime.

A tremendous sound reverberates in the sky right over our heads. He bounds into my arms and hides his face in my neck, his body tensed.

'What's that?'

'That's the thunder, darling. When the *deva*s and *asura*s fight in the sky, then you can hear thunder. They are huge, aren't they? And their *gada*s enormous. The clouds carry Indra and he throws this weapon of sound.'

'They're fighting now?'

'Yeah, a *big* fight.'

I secure his dripping body with my hand, comforting him as we meander home. I smile to myself. It is fun retelling the stories my parents had told me.

~

From where I sit, I cannot see the supine figure on the bed but I am aware of him, aware of peace. I have ushered an unexploded bomb through turbulence, safely into sleep.

I stare at the screen in front of me for a while, begin to type…

She is seated beside her husband. In front of them, their two handsome sons. The comforts of a palace surround her, costly furnishings, maids, the choicest of foods. She is dressed in silk and gold, but her inner self holds itself away, a little apart from her rich attire. She listens to them talking and at some point, her mind wanders…

That particular day, her life changed, the day she got married.

Tired after the ceremonies but exhilarated as well, a bride finally, she sat beside her husband in a chariot covered with gold while they were escorted by their clansmen. In front, reins in hand, was seated her cousin, a sign of his great affection for her. Following them, gifts from her father, chariots, horses, caparisoned elephants. Her head bent under the veil, she was admiring the henna on her hands, the wedding bangles.

Then, a voice from the heavens took her name.

Her cousin unsheathed his sword. It glinted in the sun as it flashed towards her. The unbearable pain, her scalp tight in his grasp. She was a second away from death, saved only by the quick action of her husband.

She heard him speak philosophy, talk calmly about life and death, appeal to the better nature of a panic-stricken man. It was in this unexpected way that she got to know Vasudeva. When nothing worked, he promised that he himself would hand over his children, as soon as they were born, to Kamsa.

Her life was spared.

In the following months, she thought often about the prophecy. The Lord Himself would be born to her. Her mind could not stretch around a thought so vast, condense it into the form of a baby. What had she done to merit this? She was not sure.

The eighth child. Her heart swelled with delight. That meant she would have so many children.

When she discovered she was to have a baby, she was happy, and apprehensive, like any other girl her age. The thought that hovered over her, a dark shadow, she banished from her mind.

The baby was born. A boy, their son.

They named him Kirtiman. He had a birthmark on his thigh. She had barely held the child in her arms when Vasudeva calmly took him away from her. He left her weeping for her baby.

He was smiling when he came back to the prison, the infant with him. It began to cry, it was hungry, but before she could move, Kamsa appeared at his side and snatched it away from him.

They spent years there—more than a decade in that damp, cold place—all because of a prophecy.

Strange are His ways. Why did He have to announce it; why did He have to forewarn Kamsa?

She looks across at her youngest, seated in front of her, and wants to ask him but when her eyes graze his charming face, she cannot. Something within her melts. It was all worth it, she thinks.

She remembers the day He freed them.

As He approached her, she saw the feather quivering in the breeze, the flute tucked into his waistband, the distinctive golden-yellow silk that flared around him, his smile. In an instant the shackles were gone, her feet buoyant.

She touched his cheek, in wonder, tears in her eyes. My son. Behind him, her other child, Balarama. After so many years of thirst, drought, she heard the word uttered, 'Maa'. Sweetness itself.

Gentle words he spoke to them, apologising for the distress caused to them, for the fact that Balarama and he had not served them lovingly as children would their parents. Now that Kamsa was gone, they would live together, their palaces restored to them.

Kamsa. Six times he strode into the prison chamber. Six times he held another of her babies by the legs and six times she heard the sound of something soft, barely formed dash against the wall.

The baby brought from Gokul was Yogamaya herself. Oh, the look on his face when She changed form and slipped out of his hand, told him that Krishna lived.

He, Kamsa, who had been so fond of her, verily like a brother, he who would have granted any wish of hers. It all changed so fast — grief turns her limbs into lead.

It was a friendly guard who told them what had happened after Vasudeva took his first-born to Kamsa.

Kamsa thought about what the voice in the sky had said and decided that he would spare the life of Kirtiman, the first child and of all the others, except the dreaded eighth. He had given the child back to Vasudeva, when Narada appeared in his court. It was Narada who had whispered things in his ear making him change his mind. Then Kamsa went back on his word, followed Vasudeva to the prison-chamber.

In the dark half of the month of Shravana, when the moon was in Rohini, a child emerged from her womb. She looked at it and the sun was in her eyes. When Vasudeva held the baby, he too was blinded by light. A light so brilliant, it revealed for the first time the dismal walls and far corners of their prison.

The baby had four hands and clutched an object in each of them. They were like the miniature toys she had played with as a child. He had a beautiful crown and was covered with the dazzle of jewels, of which, the one on his chest shone the brightest. He had the softest, silkiest hair on his head. His eyes were like the very petals of the lotus flower he held in his right hand.

The baby spoke, almost as though he had read her mind, in answer to her question. He had promised her that he would be born thrice as her son. Many aeons before, Vasudeva and she, then Sutapa and Prishni had lived extremely disciplined lives, sometimes eating only fallen leaves for a meal, and had completed their austerities over thousands of years. Pleased with her pure heart, her devotion to Him, He had granted her a boon: anything.

What she wanted was simple: For Him to be born as her child. Pleased even more, that wish he granted three times over, in three different lives. His birth as Krishna was the last of the three lives.

She barely heard his praise; of her past austerities, she had no recollection. Her mind was on her child. She was afraid that Kamsa would come storming in and find her baby. What gruesome method would he use this time? Full of fear, she begged the baby to assume a normal form, cloak his brilliance. She fed him, placed him in a cane basket, tucked a cloth around him to keep him warm and watched anxiously as Vasudeva walked into the night.

When Kamsa rushed towards her, she held her daughter close, would have pressed her back into the safety of her womb if that were possible. She pleaded with him. Surely a baby girl was not going to kill him? But he was mad with fear and rage, his hair and clothes in disarray. He had only one thought on his mind for his was the obsession of hatred. And yet, it was a thought that redeemed, for his mind was preoccupied with Vishnu at all times.

He tore the baby away from her, pulling it by its legs and in the same movement flipped it over, wanting to smash its head on stone. Instantly they saw the goddess ascending, gliding higher and higher above their heads. She was so beautiful! So fragrant!

One second a cruel, heartless man, the next, a man filled with remorse, asking their forgiveness. He even removed the shackles from their feet.

But, he had bad advisors.

He went back on his word, yet again. The next day, the shackles were back in place and Putana was summoned.

A thought comes to her. She hesitates a second, then turns to her sons and says, 'O Balarama, O Krishna. I heard that by your wonderful, mysterious power, you brought the son of your guru Sandipani Muni back to life. I have suffered terribly. Each time I gave birth with great hope and each time that hope was killed before my very eyes. I wish to see my sons. Once. Just once and my heart's desire will be met.'

Krishna and Balarama travel to the planet Sutala, where Bali reigns. Tears of bliss flow from Bali's eyes. He has seen his Lord once again. Once again, he offers Him everything that is his. Krishna tells him that the six dead sons, previously the sons of Hiranyakashipu, who were placed one after one in the womb of Devaki, inhabit Sutala. He wants to take them back to Devaki, give her the pleasure of cradling her children in her arms, of marvelling at their smiling faces. Once they drink from the same breast that fed Krishna himself, they will be blessed. Given back their lost status of demi-gods, they will ascend to a higher place.

Krishna transforms the six souls into babies and places them in the hands of his mother, in Dwaraka.

Devaki is overwhelmed with joy. Of her eight children, the only one she suckled was her youngest, Krishna. Briefly, just enough to keep him from hunger during that perilous journey to Gokul. And then, he too was gone.

A mother, at last, her lost babies regained. All eight of her children with her. She is rich!

There is nothing more she can wish for. Milk flows from her breasts. She first feeds Smara, whom she had named Kirtiman, then Udgitha, then Parisvanga, then Patanga, then Ksudrabhrt, and finally, Ghrni. Brothers to Krishna. Brothers to Balarama. She holds them, kisses them, cuddles them, smoothens the fine hairs on their heads, pats them to sleep in her lap, delights in their clean baby-smell, presses her finger on the dimple in their chins and makes them smile. She nuzzles them like a cow its calf. Something soft and tender unfurls in her heart, *vatsalya* – love for a child.

She lives in that moment.

I work on what I have written, refining it further.

Imperfect though it is, there is the sense of having wrested something of permanence from the day, something that will last.

~

Rice has been soaked and ground, and made into a thin watery paste. It looks like milk, a sea of white in a round plate.

I lift Sanju, dip his feet in the paste and ask him to step out of it, onto the floor, first one step, then another. Three steps later, I lift him onto the plate, wet his feet again. He wonders what it is that I am doing.

When the footprints dry completely, gleaming white against the dark floor-tile, there is the patter of tiny feet running through the house, leading straight to the freshly decorated puja. *Patram, pushpam, phalam, toyam* and for the newly born Krishna: *navaneetam.*

'How did he come?' asks Sanju. 'All by himself?'

~

Nectar in the ear

I adore the Lord's feet

whose
anklets set with gems
resound eloquently
while
along the pathways of Gokula
are scattered
dainty foot-prints.

~

A house where no one lives, an old woman without a home, it seems a perfect fit. Within a week, the entire space under the neem is hidden by layers of dry, dead leaves and one does not have to watch for her anymore while driving down the road at night. And yet, early one night, around eight o'clock, I discover Thayee sleeping in front of the gate.

I brake within inches of her. Resenting her strongly, I get out, opening the gate before she does.

'Thayee!'

She is always so accommodating when woken up, immediately making the effort to rise. My exasperation thins out by the time she is actually on her feet and out of harm's way.

'Why don't you sleep inside the compound?'

'Which compound?' her eyes squinting at the headlights.

'That house there.'

'Oh, the mosquitoes there are terrible. Great big ones. And then there are ants that bite me.'

I am annoyed with myself for coming to simple conclusions.

The next time I pass the place, one *amavasya* night when the moon renews himself, I am made aware of what it becomes when darkness aspects it. Errant rays of light from the surrounding houses fall into the black watery space contained by the road and the three shared walls. Reflected on a window pane here, the glass made live, refractive, or sliding across a tall angle of wall there, they build a hadowy island of substance, the house itself. Crickets sing, the frequently shifting body of voices providing points of reference for the ears. Everything else is submerged, spaces collapsed and rearranged, under a great flowing sea of darkness. Only memory can inform it now with daytime colour and depth.

~

With an air of finality, the driver empties the bucket on some plants that grow by the side of the road. Muddy droplets coalesce on the waxy surface of the broad leaves, sliding desultorily before collecting in the centre. He wrings the last drops of dirt from a purple cheese cloth and spreads it on the bonnet of the car to dry. The part of the road which surrounds the vehicle is wet, the tarred gravel black and glistening.

This is the other job he had contracted some months before: to wash a neighbour's brand new car early in the morning after wiping his own, the white Maruti.

The routine is disturbed however, this particular cloudy, rather pleasant morning. I have reversed the car in readiness and wait, parked in the middle of the road, for Sanju to finish his milk and come running out. We will be late for school. I worry. Forced by proximity into an awareness of the situation, I watch.

The driver is to my right, leaning over the bonnet. The wipers stand at an angle to the windscreen, like two missiles ready to fire. His entire being focussed on the point of action, to the grave exclusion of everything else, he returns those instruments gently to their state of rest.

Behind him, on the left, a young man in stylish trousers and a shiny pink shirt handles the Maruti 800, opening and slamming the doors, one by one. The car really does not need any cleaning, but he must make a favourable impression on his new employers, so he does everything with emphasis, alacrity. He takes care not to look across the narrow road, hiding his embarrassment in these busy, slightly nervous, movements. Besides, it is too soon for the intimacy of sympathy.

I honk once, to summon Sanju. The sound bursts forth startling both the men who turn briefly in my direction and then away.

The driver replaces the bucket in Fatima's courtyard, partly from habit, partly from an unwillingness to completely renounce hope. He is dressed in a cotton shirt and a lungi with small checks in blue and green. The skullcap, formally embroidered, is spotless. He is saving his good clothes.

He peels the damp cloth off the car and stuffs it into a bag made of colourful plastic wires knotted to a pattern. A bottle of liquid cleaner sticks out over the rim. He picks up the bag, the pliant handles safe within his palm, and walks past me, back straight, the bearded face gaunt with the strain of maintaining composure. His eyes, not entirely hidden by his steel-framed spectacles, give him away though. There is distress in them, the ache of the dispossessed, and the understanding that suddenly he is only a car-cleaner.

~

Sanju is charging up the stairs when he hits his shin against the step. I hear a cry and run, mad with fear at how bad it might be. The skin has not broken, but there is a swelling. He is howling, partly from pain, partly from apprehension about the care. I apply ice and his cry ascends to an even louder wail. He will not let me touch the area, is kicking and pushing my hands away now.

Appa tries to help but Sanju wants only me. The bulge on his leg is bigger; it needs more ice. His wails penetrate my head, scramble my brain. I want to cry. Sit in one place, lean against something solid, and cry.

A week later, he is running up the stairs when he hits his shin in the same swollen place.

~

That divinity abiding in every being in the form of race,
I bow my head before Her, again and again and again
and yet again.

That divinity abiding in every being in the form of shame,
I bow my head before Her, again and again and again
and yet again.

Her eyes are fixed in single-minded concentration; a steady, unwavering gaze that devolves on the *asura*, brings him to his death. Her many hands are raised, countless weapons in them. Select gifts: a conch, a discus, an axe, a noose, a trident, a sword, a bow, a mace. A bell from Airavata. Arms radiating from both sides of her bejewelled, astonishingly beautiful body. And yet, the face is benign, the primary right hand bestowing freedom from fear — *abhaya,* and the left granting all wishes — *varada*. Roses and marigolds garland her — statuesque dazzle of light emerged from gods several, long hair loose about her shoulders. At her feet, part buffalo, part demon, Mahishasura lies vanquished, caught in the penultimate state before he is beheaded.

Tvaiyaitat dharyate visvam tvayaitat srijyate jagat tvayaitat palyate devi tvamatsyante cha sarvada...

By You supported this universe, by You created this world, by You protected O Devi, and consumed at the end...

The priest waves the multi-flamed *arati* in front of her and the sound of the *dhak* seizes the pulse of everyone in the *pandal*. At first it is slow, an attenuated beat of eight, the emphasis placed at the end. Incense burned over coal and fibre spills smoke into the crowded room. There is no breeze, the windows are shut.

People press upon each other, runnels of sweat flowing off the forehead and neck. The women are dressed in their finest, to honour her — this daughter come home to her parents, to rest her drooping head on her mother's silken shoulder. She will stay only for nine days, for Shiva is lost without his Shakti, and must leave on the tenth. Refreshed, she will gather once again her tremendous and fearful energies, be mother to all of creation. The collective accommodates a man forging his way in at one end, dislodges someone else at another, heads reorient their positions in order to see her better.

Visrishtau srishtirupa tvam stithirupa cha palane tatha samhrti rupante jagato'sya jaganmaye...

O Devi of a form pervading the whole world, at the time of creation Your form is one of creative force; when sustaining it Your form is that of a protective energy; and at the time of dissolution Your form is one with the destructive power.

The lone priest stands in front of the *Devi*, child-like, looking up at her. His arm waves a lotus, swirling, dancing with a delicate movement of the wrist. A woman blows continuously on the conch, the eerie, piercing cry of victory. His hand clasps a sari, an undulating offering to the goddess. The beat of the drums is quicker, the emphasis on every fourth and eighth beat, the pauses painted, filled with sound.

120

The bare arm of the priest raises a single-flamed *arati* to her; she of the plump cheeks and large, expressive eyes. The *dhak* beats faster, closer, three beats rushing into the space meant for two.

The flames are borne towards the assembly. Myriad hands reach out, jostling for the warmth of blessing. Someone fans the incense and smoke envelops both goddess and devotees in a thick cloud—a surreal atmosphere.

She has brought her young with her. Lakshmi and Ganesh, Saraswati and Kartikeya. They surround her but are unbelievably obedient. They do not leave the places assigned to them, nor do they squirm. They like the attention, the food offered with such love on their annual visit. A banana tree stands beside them, drooping herald of their arrival.

The pace is identical with the heartbeat; the heart expands and throbs to its sound. It is short, every stroke emphasised. The *dhaki*, his *dhak* slung to one side, is unaware of his power. Thoughts flee the mind, as a single radiant image pervades it. *Durgati Harini*, Destroyer of Evil Tendencies. A filament spins itself out from each of us and is held in his grasp. He reels us in tight, tighter. Palms fold humbly, eyes bow.

The ceiling fans start all of a sudden and they whir to rhythm as well. Surely, he cannot go faster than this; the heart cannot bear such strain. A hand raises a silver oxtail fan with redolent *oguru* sprinkled on it, an attempt to cool the Goddess, soothe her after the great fight. The *dhak* relents, the heart beats with ease and with three conclusive taps, the battle is won.

*Mahavidya mahamaya mahamedha mahasmrtih mahamoha
cha bhavati mahadevi mahasuri...*

You are supreme knowledge and great illusion too, great intellect, great contemplation and great delusion are You, Mighty Goddess and Mighty Asuri too…

People turn the other way, surge towards the *prasad*. A few dreamers remain, gazing in awe at her very real presence. They know that the nine nights of festivity are not only a matter of the just completed ritual. In essence, they are a celebration of human attributes embodied by the Goddess; a celebration of human life. Hunger and thirst are natural attributes of being human, as are energy and sleep. The same mind that is intelligent and capable of reflection also has the capacity to mislead and delude.

Shame and delusion, contentment and good fortune, are all parts of life, not to be spurned. That is what one celebrates here today.

Somewhere on her crown, a diamond catches light and sparkles in the mist. Near the door, the *dhaki* sits on a chair, emptied, no longer wearing his *dhak*. He is drenched in sweat.

A heart-wrenching separation lies ahead, stained with the red of sindoor. Tomorrow, she will leave her father's tender care; dissolve in the ever-journeying waters of the sea.

~

The bitter-sweet indulgence of nostalgia.

I remember the last time my guru taught me something new, remember the colour of a *varnam*. The puja had just ended. A mountain of ripe fruits and coconuts lay in front of the deities. Their forms were submerged in a bright sea of flowers hidden by the thick swirling mist of incense. The long-awaited moment; suspense and its satisfaction — what would Sir teach us? Tradition dictated that we began learning anew the day Goddess Saraswati was venerated.

Great excitement on hearing the words *'Uma sutam'*, disbelief at our good luck. The words and their meaning were familiar, as was the choreography. The entire Ganesha *varnam* had permeated into the bloodstream. I had watched it so many times being performed by him. And yet, even though I knew the *mudra*s that flowed one after one, even though I knew the stories being narrated, I could not actually dance it, not having received it directly from him.

Did he really think we were ready for it?

Were we?

The morning after Vijayadashami, when Sir actually began to teach the *varnam*, I followed him in movement with a sense of bemusement. It was as though he had just given each of us a rare and precious jewel, very casually, without ceremony and I held that priceless, glowing, iridescent stone, looking at it in disbelief as it shone in my palms. Right foot, then left foot struck in the very first movement a little leap and two hands blossomed into a flowery circle that ended in the ear and trunk of Ganesha. The movements were complicated not because they were difficult to execute, but because they were different and unusual.

Time now flowed to the fundamental beat of eight. That first day, the first *jathi,* took an entire hour to grasp and remember. *Uma sutam,* one described him with happy fingers, now the flapping ears, now the swaying trunk, with only one prayer inside, that he may not place any obstacles in the way of my learning the *varnam,* for his praise would only be complete in reaching the end of it.

I left the class exhausted, my clothes dark with sweat but there was a sense of exhilaration, of having been jet-thrusted into an atmosphere of great and endless joy.

The next day, I was so intent on completing the first *jathi* and the *abhinaya* that followed, so wildly enthusiastic in my execution, that there were no reserves of energy left for learning the second *jathi.* Dismay! I understood then that dance is really about conserving energy, about finding a way to expend it in an even manner, so that it lasts through the length of the *varnam.*

Over the next few days, amazingly, the time it took to complete a *jathi* shrunk, and so did my mental image of it. What had once seemed overwhelmingly long and very tiring was now compressed, and what had once taken an effort to even understand was danced away in five minutes.

Passing through the gateway of music and dance, I left behind the ordinary world of time, of hours and minutes and mealtimes. No sooner had I left my footwear by the entrance and walked barefoot into dance class than the personal, the mundane, fell away and I slipped into a far more magical and yet very real world.

I watched in awe as my guru became Parvati, saw the playful ease with which she created a child in a second, participated in the joy of self-discovery felt by that youth, the earnestness with which he undertook the task of guarding the wondrous being who was his mother, and then beheld Shiva who could not comprehend how a young boy, a stranger, dared come in the way of his seeing his beloved wife. I was caught in that terrible moment of anger which led through destruction to the creation of an even more endearing being, an elephant-headed creature, with a human body and a heavy ponderous gait who perceived in his father and mother the entire universe.

An effervescence of emotions, immense, evanescent, was registering on the fluid, mobile surface of my guru's face. One can never tire of gazing at it. It was this face, these expressions, *bhava*, that I bravely mirrored with my own, knowing that I could only try.

One begins a *varnam* as one would a journey, knowing that there is a point of departure and a time of return. What kind of madness is it that draws one repeatedly into making this journey of dance, of creating an entire universe with one's body as it moves in time through space, knowing that at the end there will be nothing tangible to show for it, except the memory of the journey itself? Many repetitions later, I had absorbed the *varnam* into my body. The words and their meanings were now lent to *mudra*s of the left and right hands, just as the *swara*s were given a definite shape by the bodylines of movements stitched together.

The *raga* Naata-kurinji acquired newer, lasting associations. From then on, it had woven into it the gentle October sunshine and the gold-green of the coconut leaves, visible from the window. It had the image of Sir sitting in front of us, intent on transmitting learning; his face reflecting every movement that we made while we in turn drew on his approval to continue. It contained within it all the time I had spent in that very same classroom, the span of childhood and the later years. It was silk off the loom of the singer's voice, serene, strong, leading me firmly to those feelings that were to be expressed in *abhinaya*.

Then came the day when Sir completed teaching us the *varnam*. We had learnt it, committed it to memory.

That day, when I checked my watch for the time and rushed back to everyday life, something had changed forever: I now knew the Ganesha *varnam*.

~

On Friday, it was a rain holiday. Then there was the weekend and the Puja holidays. This Vijayadashami, my guru was not in town, and so we haven't learnt anything new. The day has draped itself tightly over me like some fine-clinging fabric, giving me no room to breathe. I crave the order of the weekdays for those three-and-a-half hours of school, and nested within them the hour I spend dancing, that are like a support, an inner framework, a scaffolding that holds up this fabric of the day and keeps it from collapsing on me.

'Maa, I am seeing my cupboard, okay?'

It is afternoon and he is charged.

We are in our room, a prison for the next two hours until it is time for tiffin. The upper part of the door is held firmly with the bolt. When the idea of escape strikes him, he will use the handle, banging the door repeatedly with the limited negotiation of the lower half, where the key does not turn fully in the lock. To prevent that I must keep him amused for I am the guardian of sounds while my parents sleep.

'Okay!'

He pulls out a gun and his toy cars.

They clatter to the floor one by one. I close my eyes while he plays with them, accompanying them on the highway with a soundtrack of speed.

'Whee! Duzh! Zoom! Crash!'

When he is around, there is no quietude.

I conserve energy only to find myself expending it on unproductive things; repeating myself constantly, answering the same question five times over. To try and think through the noise and his voice pitched high is another way to tiredness.

I wake up with a sense of fright—why is he so quiet?—find him searching for an oddly shaped piece, scratching his elbow where a mosquito has bitten him. It is a rare day, when he gets involved with his puzzles and makes them serially, seated on the floor.

I doze off.

After a while, I am aware, held within sound, my eyes closed against the light. Puzzles done, he is pulling other toys out of the cupboard.

Barely one hour has passed.

He has seen the cupboard and tired of its contents. I get up from the bed and step on devastation. A tornado has swept across the room. On the floor, a series of cartoon characters framed in mosaic, cars involved in multiple collisions, a dog without a tail, Lego pieces magnanimously freed from their containers, a tail, cotton foaming out of it, a beautiful plane built entirely from his imagination and pieces of assorted plastic strewn everywhere. Having found an Erinmore tin filled with foreign coins, he is trying to open it. The coins burst out of the tin and birl under the bed heading in all eight directions.

He opens the chest of drawers. Maybe I will have to wait till Sanju is grown up and married, with children, before I can dance. What if life is an obstacle race, and the prize, space and solitude in which to think? Will I have to bring up my grandchildren as well, before I can finally get the prize?

He wears one T-shirt, then another, and another over that one, giggling all the while. He knows by the way I am watching him that I am not amused.

Five pairs of shorts float up his legs in a similar way. Clothes spill out of the yawning drawer as he searches impatiently for something. He finds his underpants and settles them on his head. He is dressed. He turns from the mirror, a fierce moustache pencilled on his lip.

There is a mass of snakes crawling across my skull.

This sense of defeat is entirely rooted in the context of my personality, and his, set at the intersection of place and time. It is of no help to observe other mothers with their much quieter children, they probably have their own problems.

Half an hour to tea.

~

To the left of Palani's thatched hut is a drumstick tree. It stands to one side of the road, on public property. During the rainy season, the tree is laden. The long stem-like fruits resemble scores of green snakes hanging from the tree.

In happier times, Thayee would have casually inserted a branch broken from someone's garden into the ground, packing earth tightly around it so that it stood straight. A plaster of cow-dung applied to the top of the wounded limb would have sealed in vital moisture.

For many days, it would have looked like a pole on which someone had placed a ball of fly infested, smelly dung. Then, overnight, a shoot pregnant with leaves would have escaped from the dry bark of the stump, and another, and then another. Miraculously almost, the sinuous, tapered fruit would have appeared. A long rope at first, filling out over time into snakes swinging rigidly, heads nailed to the branch.

Since then, Thayee has lost her home, her privileges, her tree. Her daughter-in-law uses a long bamboo pole with an iron hook to harvest the fruit from the branches, and frightens her neighbours who attempt theft.

When Thayee wanders down the road, she knows each tree and shrub by its use. The edible leaves of the drumstick, an innocuous store of iron. She would steam the small, rounded leaves and garnish them with grated coconut.

Now she cannot remember the last time she cooked a meal.

She divides the broad, thick leaf of the banana with a precise stroke of the knife and a disposable plate falls into her hand. The karuvepellai produces nothing but aromatic leaves essential for seasoning, and the flowering neem, the tree of forty cures, is life itself. The fronds of the coconut rarely come crashing down; she has to wait until someone calls the tree-climber.

For a snack, she usually plucks bare the karuvepellai shrub in our garden.

When the oil is hot and the mustard is popping, at that critical second when the leaves are a must for flavour, Amma dashes out to the backyard and discovers the denuded plant.

She suspects caterpillars but detects the culprit soon enough.

Thayee is not around to hear the scolding.

~

I am irritated. Sanju will not eat. He will argue about everything. He will resist, resist, resist till I am drained of all energy.

I say to him, 'Someday you will have a baby and I hope that baby bugs you and troubles you the same way you are troubling me!'

'It won't trouble me. It will trouble the mamma.'

~

When two people meet, their histories meet.

I discover continually how different Murthy's and mine are. A mother and father who dote on me, gift me the wealth of a happy childhood, make me secure in their love, present to me a world that is good, and fair and filled with love. This is what I bring with me, my innocence, and my happy world. Why wouldn't I be loved the way I already am?

The shock then of learning that he is too self-contained, warped in a way that thwarts examination — to need a wife. So well-hidden is it by polite manners and smiles that most people think he is a mild-mannered, good-natured person.

I realise now that I married my own assumptions of marriage, imagined that they were his as well: affection reciprocated, love for the other's company, a future made prosperous by co-operation and understanding — 'Everyday's most quiet need'.

In all those hours I spent with Murthy before we married, how much did I truly get to know about him?

Dry, queer, without an iota of affection in them, they fit each other — parents and son. In their history of misguided, restrictive parenting and a damaged growing child, they are the cause and effect, linked forever in a cycle of warped guidance and warped becoming. Where do I, from a radiant, happy world, belong in this?

Should I mourn his distance from his child or should I rejoice that he is too far away to hurt my child with his whimsical attention?

~

I approach the gate to find Thayee sitting in front of it, dead-centre—where the two panels are held together by the latch. She hugs her knees close to her chest, legs crossed at the ankles. The stick leans against the gate-post.

I pause and look down at her, waiting for her to move so that I can enter my home.

'Thayee?'

'Aaahn?'

'Thayee…'

She turns her head so that her ear faces me.

'*Kadhe sevade'mma.*'

She never tires of saying that. A deep furrow runs all the way down the side of her nose to her chin. Minute warts, darker than the skin on her face, dot the creased surface of her cheek. Her hair is open, untidy, like baby serpents massed together, tails resting at various points on her shoulder.

'*Von peru yenna?*'

'Aaahn?' She frowns, having heard the question but unsure that she has actually heard right.

'*Peru.* Your name?'

She lifts her chin to look at me. Her brow smoothens. A queer light shines in her eyes. 'Balammal,' she says, articulating a sound that she hasn't heard in years. 'But you can call me *kezhavi,* the old hag. I won't mind. That's what everyone calls me.'

Smiling, I shake my head in disagreement and walk away from her towards the front door. She has settled down on the ground again; I can hear a pleased chuckle from behind the gate.

~

Many coconuts have matured on the trees. Some fall at night, I hear them: a sudden thud, now familiar, that disrupts a dream. When Amma wanders around her garden in the morning, she stumbles on a coconut, exclaiming delightedly as though she has found a half-buried treasure. She bears it triumphantly away to the storeroom at the back, pleased, of course, that her garden has yielded a prize but especially thrilled that it has escaped Thayee's nocturnal, roving eyes.

More coconuts fall. The trees have become top-heavy, swaying wildly with the wind and Amma worries that a coconut may fall on Sanju's head. When the tree-climber calls at the gate, Amma has a job for him.

'How much for four trees?'

It becomes difficult to agree on a reasonable wage once the work has been done, and the haggling can get quite intense and acrimonious.

The remuneration is acceptable. He moves swiftly to the first tree he sees. Frog-legged, feet splayed around it, he draws himself up the slender trunk. A stout coir belt holds his feet together, and in place. The checked loin-cloth he wears just about covers his thin, undernourished hips. A basket made of dried coconut husk in which he carries a sickle, dangles by his side. When he comes down the road calling his trade, he is recognised by that pale brown basket and the coir belts looped over his shoulder, by the way he walks with his eyes lifted sideways, searching for coconuts against the sky.

Finally, he has reached the top and straightens himself, under the umbrella-like cluster of fronds, leaning against the other belt that secures him at waist-level to the tree.

From below, it looks as though the straight trunk has branched into a limb at the very top.

He works without hesitation, knowledgeably. The sharp metal half-moon severs the curly umbilical cords and a storm of coconuts comes thudding down around us, bouncing sometimes before rolling to a stop. He hacks at the base of an enormous frond and we duck when it falls to earth like a piece of green sky. The bark of the trunk bears the mark of each of the fronds that grew and were cut away. The scars are like blank eyes, wide in the middle, tapering horizontally to an end.

The history of those dead leaves is imprinted indelibly on the body of the tree.

When he is done, the garden looks as though a cyclone has struck. The fronds lie about like giant corpses, their several leafy arms twisted beneath them. Some have fallen unavoidably on top of the delicate bushes and shrubs Amma has planted in her garden. The man lifts them, one by one and drags them onto the road where he dumps them, just outside our wall.

That stack of leaves represents a whole roof or part of it at least. Alternately, those numerous arms hide within them a precious marrow, the broomstick. Already, two women have moved into position just beyond the gate, waiting to take them away before anyone else does.

Where is Thayee?

The harvest of fruit has to be secured in the storeroom and the man makes several trips, holding four or five at a time by the wiry stem that remains at the base. Soon, a green-gold sea of coconuts covers the floor.

He has one last task to perform; the one Sanju has been looking forward to. He squats on the driveway and wipes the tip of his sickle with a leaf. Deftly, with three clean strokes, he hacks away part of the husk of a tender coconut and the inner husk is revealed, the coconut now two-toned, green where the husk remains, off-white where it has been prepared.

The skin on his hands is tough, punished by the weather and circumstances. He is not muscular but the muscles of his bare torso lie clearly defined below the ebony skin, close to the bone.

This patient, almost painstaking effort to reach the nourishment hidden inside the coconut fascinates me every time I see it; it is a magic that never pales.

I have already given him the vessel and with a dramatic flourish he taps at the shell with the tip of his sickle and forces open a circular hatch. He up-ends the coconut onto the vessel and lets it rest there while the sweet, clear water gushes out. Then he wedges the sickle deep into the husk and bangs the coconut on the cement until it splits open to reveal the creamy, translucent, nascent flesh.

A cut at the side of the shell and he has prepared a spoon. Here he slows down, bringing all his concentration to bear on what he is doing. Carefully, he works the spoon into the delicate membrane, moving it away from the shell, and then scoops it out into the dish I have placed before him. It takes me a while and much observation to understand that he is trying hard not to touch the soft pulp with his unclean hand.

A short length of cloth is wrapped around his head. He is younger than Thayee, but like her, there is no spare flesh on his face, and the skin clings hungrily to the contours of his skull.

Amma hands me the money to give to him. I look at the notes rolled into a cylinder and unfold them. Forty rupees: ten per tree. Isn't it too little for all the work he has done? I turn to ask Amma and then decide against it. I know already what she will say: 'To give too much is to be taken for a fool, to open oneself to exploitation. A deal is a deal after all and he is not complaining, is he?'

There is some hidden balance, some intricate calculation that is maintained in this sort of transaction and I know I will never understand it.

He stands at a distance, crouching within himself, his gaze directed downwards as he holds his hand out respectfully. I place the notes in his palm and ask myself if there isn't something I can give him other than money? The only thing I can think of is an unopened packet of glucose biscuits and I catch up with him at the gate to give it to him. Surprised, he drops it into the basket beside the sickle and walks out onto the road. Barefoot.

I look up. The trees, shorn of their drooping, out-spread fronds, look unattractive and the light has changed. Instead of a ribboned sky and strained, mellow sunlight, there is now light everywhere, bright, uniform and the sky is blue in its immensity. A crow glides from tree to tree, confused, looking for its accustomed perch. It settles temporarily on the telephone pole.

The driveway is littered with miniature stunted coconuts and gauze-like fibre from the tops of the trees. Near the lemon tree, there is a crooked pile of half-shells and a slice of husk that passes for a spoon. In the backyard, the storeroom has been bolted and a strong lock placed on it.

~

We have more coconuts than we need, so Amma decides to sell some of them. A message is sent to Palani's wife. There is an advantage here for both of them. Amma has a ready buyer for which convenience she is willing to sell them cheap, wholesale. As for that woman, she will buy them, de-husk them and sell them in the market for double the price she has paid for them.

In the afternoon, the bell rings. I have finished clearing the table and am about to go in search of Thayee. Plate in hand, I open the door thinking it is the postman. It is Palani's wife; she has come for the coconuts. She stands near the gate, her face like a dark smiling moon. She is unusually fat. Unusual, because the other women in the area, who work as maids or iron clothes, are thin as much from poverty as overwork. The sleeves of her blouse are tight, riding high above bulging flesh. She has five children; the eldest recently had a baby and the youngest is about nine years old.

I walk past her, calling out to Amma as I go out.

Thayee is not in front of the empty house. Disappointed, I ask the day watchman, 'Where is Thayee?' He is certain that she is inside the compound but refuses to look for her.

'Since the day the Bhai took her coconuts, I have not spoken to her,' he says, politely, apologetically even. His hair gleams; oil maintains it together neatly, away from the straight, accurate parting on the left. He has a thin moustache and small eyes. To show that he means no disrespect to me, he walks across the road and peering over the wall, locates her instantly.

She is asleep, lying just inside, near the gate, in the shade of the wall. She wakes up with a start. A wreath of red hibiscus flowers decorates her forehead. She has stuffed them under the rag turban she ties sometimes over her head. I think she does it for the cooling effect they might have. I have always wanted to ask her but have put it off until I can find the energy to shout.

She sees the drumsticks, like flat catamarans in the sea of sambar, and mumbles.

Doesn't she like drumsticks? Will she not eat them?

'What?' I ask her. 'What about the drumsticks?'

'You can eat them plain,' she says before becoming indistinct again. She speaks in a dialect that I do not always understand. 'Chop a few onions, fry them brown, add salt and chillies…'

A recipe. Thayee is giving me a recipe. I smile to myself.

'I'll come sometime and show you how to do it,' she says and I wonder if she has woken properly from her sleep.

Palani's wife stands in the shade, still at the gate, waiting for Amma. Behind her, the oleander, thanga arali, is alight with flowers, and the scattering of yellow flowers beneath it, is like its own reflection in the black mirror of the road. She watches me walk towards her.

'Where's your son?' she asks.

'He's inside, why?'

'You were carrying the food. I thought you were feeding him.'

The opportunity I have been waiting for! Not wasting a second, 'I went to feed your mother-in-law,' I say witheringly and look to see what effect my words have on her.

She looks at me blankly, even holds my disapproving gaze for a fleeting brazen moment. And then there is nothing to say.

Amma calls out to her, asking her to come around to the back, to the storeroom. Later, from my window, I watch as she drags away a gunny bag filled with the coconuts, walking the short distance to her home. After she has taken the last load, Amma shuts the gate behind her. Noticing me, she sings, 'Not bad! I made eighty-three rupees.' Her saplings have grown into money! Nothing gives Amma so much pleasure as these odd, infrequent bits of income earned from selling coconuts or drumsticks and, of course, the old newspapers, magazines and ketchup bottles. Palani's wife has no money to pay for what she has bought though, and until she sells them at a profit, Amma must remain a creditor.

~

'*Bhagavaan* is everywhere and in everything, *kanna*.'
'He is in me also?' He is lying in my arms, looking up at me.
'Yes.'
'Where?'
'Inside your heart.' I tap his chest. 'Here.'
'And inside that *Bhagavaan's* heart?'
'There's *Bhagavaan*.'
'And inside *that Bhagavaan's* heart?'
'He is within him as well.'
'And inside *that* heart?'

He's got the point. I must divert him or this will never end. I tickle him, kiss him to distraction.

~

On the television, a woman is being interviewed. Her child disappeared one evening; vanished from a small city in the north. None of the neighbours in the crowded, cramped locality could recall having seen her seven year-old girl after a point in time. The police could not trace her either. She has been missing for two months.

She does not sob, she does not wail, but a continuous stream of tears mars her face. She wears a stunned look that haunts me for the rest of the day.

I think of a story drawn around these meagre facts. I dream, immerse myself in this situation, try to put it in words. I want to add to it something of my own.

What if she was a very loving mother but also a tired mother? What if she had the cooking to do, the clothes to wash, the uniforms to iron, a possessive, suspicious husband and two children to manage?

In the middle of the chaos that is her life, the child demands to be let out to play.

'*Ma.*'

Other children are outside. She has finished his homework, why not let her go?

'*Ma!*'

Her elder daughter, elder by three years, has gone for tuition or she would have sent them out together. Manjari is the quiet one, Sargam, troublesome.

If she keeps Sargam inside, she will drive her mad. At the same time, she never lets her go out alone. She always keeps an eye on her.

'Maa!!!' Distracted, I mutter something, *'Umm.'*
'Why is the bus bigger than the car?'
Startled out of the story, I say, *'Hunh? What bus? What?'*
'Bus! The green bus, why is it bigger than our car?'
'Because. Just because. Go make a puzzle.'
I girdle my mind, start again:

Today, she is tired.

She wants to be free of her cares for a while. If Sargam goes out to play, she can finish her work quicker.

She has her periods. Her body aches. Yielding to the temptation of the easy, she nods grudgingly, says 'Yes.'

She makes chhole. She kneads the dough for the bhaturas covers it and sets it aside. She looks out every now and then from the window. Things seem okay, children are playing in the park.

She feels like making a raita, starts grating a cucumber to go with the curds.

'Maa.' Peace can only be known in its absence.
'Maa! Potty!' The little flat is hers, all hers.
'Ammaaa!!!'
'WHAT?'
'Potty aachu. Come clean me.'
I clean him; make him wear a fresh pair of shorts. I wash my hands and return to writing.

She can concentrate on the work at hand, she doesn't have to answer all her questions. Pay attention to her. Peace. She washes dishes, sorts out some clothes from an untidy pile and switches on the iron. She can hear children playing.

'Maa. Where is my pencil?'

She abandons worry for an hour, even has time to massage oil into her long hair.

When her husband is away at work, her self expands to the size of the flat, owns everything. Her spirit is light. Suddenly, she catches sight of the time. Her eyes run the length of the road as she leans over the balcony, looking left, then right for a group of children. Have they all gone home?

Why has *she* not come back?

She locks the door and walks towards the park searching for her. 'Sar-gam!' She is not to be seen anywhere. Anxiety mounts within her. She tries all the homes of the people with whom they are on friendly terms. 'She's not here.' The homes of her friends. 'No Auntyji. When we came home she was still playing.' Her heart is beating very fast, sweat pouring down her back. From a tentative, half-authoritative tone, her voice changes to a trembling scream. 'SAR-GAM!'

She does not give up, walks further, and further, searching places they have never seen, did not even know existed in their locality. Her georgette dupatta keeps slipping off, irritating her. She ties the ends in a rough knot, taking bigger, more frantic strides.

She *has to be* here somewhere. Another step, another turn, and she will see her. What is she wearing? Through the fog in her head, she recollects the colour. Red salwar, printed kameez. Yes. The set bought last Diwali.

'Maa! Look! I drew a plane.'
'Umm. Very good, kanna, *make another one for me. Please?'*

She is feeling sick, her stomach churns. She looks up at the terraces. She sees dozens of antennas haphazardly placed, clothes flapping in the breeze.

No sign of Sargam. Her fault. It is all her fault.

A thought crosses her mind and she runs home. Maybe she is waiting for her there. The padlocked door stares forbiddingly at her. Her hands are ice-cold. There is a sound behind her. 'Thank God,' she thinks, anger and irritation and relief exploding in her as she turns to give her the scolding of her life.

Only, it is Manjari back from Maths tuition.

Finally, it percolates; Sargam is missing.

Her husband hurries back from work and the first thing he says is, 'What sort of a mother are you? You must have been relaxing inside, stuffing yourself while she was being kidnapped. You don't look after the house at all!'

The brief moment of leisure gone, she pays for it with the rest of her life. The shock of…

I have just unravelled a thread of thought regarding the husband. It is exciting, a discovery.

'Maa!!!' He screams right into my ear. Yanked out of my reverie, I drop it. Evaporated, vanished, two books of thoughts lost to the word *'Maa'*.

142

If this story is ever completed, ever published, people reading it will negotiate printed, tactile words. No one will know about the invisible punctuation buried in the sentences.

~

The fall begins. Dust flows off smothered leaves. Strong winds whip the fronds of the coconut upwards like a scorpion's tail. The sky is grey even though it is night and lightning paints it silver in flashes. Shadows tremble, trying to hold water in the palms of their leaves. The rain is intimate with the flavour of earth— *mann vasanai*.

In the morning, the leaves on the jasmine creeper are sparkling clean and the flowers are turgid, plump with moisture. Some of the petals are bruised. I pluck five for puja.

~

That divinity abiding in every being in the form of peace,
I bow my head before Her, again and again and again
and yet again.

That divinity abiding in every being in the form of deep faith,
I bow my head before Her, again and again and again
and yet again.

Under the cover of pre-dawn darkness, there has been the noise of festivity, bombs going off endlessly, the rapid patter of the common variety, red cylinders strung together in a row and the sporadic blast of the louder, more expensive ones. The thick, unstable dome of sound collapses into the smoky debris of silence only around ten thirty.

The road is littered with concave bits of paper, red and white, spent rockets, and crushed *chakra*s, their white undersides bruised, blackened when they were set on fire. Here and there inch-high volcanoes stand spent, a miniature crater at the peak. People, tired from their early morning exertions, have vanished from the street.

I walk across to her. 'Where were you, Thayee? I came looking for you.'

'I went to Kasturi Nagar,' she waves her arm, indicating a short distance. 'The lady there gave me a sari. She gives me one every Deepavali.' Calmly, she adds, 'She said I might not be alive next year so...'

I have seen the sari the woman gave Thayee last year. The cotton is of a fine count and the cloth light. It has a tiny self-print, like a splendid secret woven into the fabric. When

Thayee wears it, drawing it out from the bag hidden behind the bush in our backyard, the white startles with its purity, conferring on her some of its lustre.

Pleased to be giving her something different, I hold the bag of delicacies ahead of me. She receives it silently, eyes fixed on the bag. Her fingers move over the crinkled plastic surface and locate the opening. Her nails are large, man-like and tough. Dirt seals the cracks along their broken edges.

She walks slowly away from me, facing the sun. Light plays with the thin material she wears, passing easily through the length that falls between her legs, impeded elsewhere by flesh; her legs frame a transparent, arched window of cloth. I can see through to them. Skinny, bowed, they meet at a point, the stark cleft from where she gave birth to four children.

It is evening at last. Scores of *diya*s and cup-candles line walls, parapets, verandahs and even sunshades. Brick and cement fronting the street are transformed, drawing the eye to the continuous waver of light along the flat ledges. The wind plays light-heartedly with the tiny flames, winning sometimes, losing against the more determined. Surely the Goddess's heart is already won. Who could resist such beauty?

Sanju waits for me to place some candles. Then in a second, he has snatched a few and runs off with them to make his own row. The coloured wax in the shiny foil appeals to him more than the messy oil-lamps. Besides they are easier to carry.

A bomb explodes. He claps his hands over his ears and runs to me. He wants protection for his ears. Amused, I fashion a turban for him with a dupatta, bandaging his ears with each fold. He puts my palms over the cloth, holds them where his ears are, and we walk towards the street joined in this odd fashion. He sees a friend and slips out from between my hands, charging straight to the middle of the road where another bomb has been lit. The fuse is glowing.

'*Sanjay!*'

He dances insouciantly back.

Children from other homes waft slowly towards us. Some have emptied their treasury of fireworks, some carry bags, itinerant pyromaniacs. Urchins from the other end of the street draw nearer, diffidently.

Sanju holds a sparkler to the heat of the flame. It sputters and lights up instantly.

'Your sleeve, watch your sleeve!' I yell.

He shouts with joy. '*Maa,* look! *Ma-aa-a!*' The heated tip moves like a magician's wand, weaving red patterns in the air. The children wave their sparklers with glee. They are too close to each other. There are incandescent iron rods and a shower of sparks everywhere. It is amazing no one is hurt as yet.

I watch him constantly. He is too trusting of the world, rushing headlong into hazard. A child's paradise of fireworks has revealed its other dimension to me. My eyes roam a frequency of sounds, alert to the slightest disaster. Why did I buy so many flowerpots and rockets? I should have remained faithful to sparklers and snake pellets. I cannot wait till the boxes are empty and we have made a bonfire of them.

Thayee emerges from the spooky, unlit compound. She is wearing rags again. Standing at the edge of darkness, she watches silver sparks burst into flower, a spray of rubies, gold and emeralds arch across the sky.

~

The weekend: time to give him a head-bath. I carry a vessel of hot water from the kitchen to the bathroom and pour it into the bucket.

I tug at his shorts. He is being silly, bending his knees when he should straighten them; refusing to step out of the crumpled clothing encircling his feet. When I lift him into the air, he hooks his toe into the shorts and they rise with him. Finally, he is naked. The marvel of a child's body: the folds of baby fat around his thighs have vanished, he is angular, spare. I hug him, my little sky-clad ascetic.

Holding his arm to prevent him from moving, I wet his hair. He cannot keep still. This is a bath, after all. It is fun. He shakes his head and the shampoo streaks to one side, wasted on an ear. I try to wipe it off while he jumps up and down, turning all the while. I aim for his head but end up lathering his cheek. I hold his head and he twirls beneath my hand. Finally, the scalp is clean. I pour water to wash the shampoo off. He ducks and the water splashes on me.

Another round of shampoo and his non-stop hopping and turning. Water pours off his lean body, oil gleaming on caramel limbs. His hair, flattened by the weight of water, is pasted to his forehead. He looks different. Dewy, delectable, his face relaxed.

I am drenched. I wrap a towel around him, but since he will not cooperate, it goes around his arms as well. I can see where the sun has touched his neck, coloured it, a brown stalk rising out of the light sand of his chest. I tell this warm towelled bundle to go upstairs where his clothes have been left behind.

A minute.

I need a minute to recover. The wet edge of my nightie hangs heavy and limp about my feet.

A bang as loud as a bomb.

I rush to the steps.

He lost his balance and his arms imprisoned within the towel could not break free in time. He fell face first on a step and now there is a cut in the centre of his forehead. It does not bleed but the skin is open, a sightless eye. Hospital it is again. He is crying. There are worms sticking out of my head. I can't leave the house like this! I have to change my clothes.

Why are these things happening to him? Is he safe nowhere? I ask again for his pain to be conveyed to me. This way both of us suffer.

At the hospital, his name is permanent in the computer. The fluorescent lighting makes everything seem cold, remote. Even the visitors sitting docilely in wide chairs are pale, bleached clean by lavender coloured light.

In the emergency room, the plastic surgeon who sewed his cut lip examines his handiwork with detached pride. The stitches are hardly visible, white against the red of tender lip. One has to know where to look. He suggests super glue for the cut. No stitches. We are to see him after a week. The nurses prepare a bandage while I promise Sanju ice cream.

~

My head is bleeding from within. If I could, I would detach it, leave it somewhere. I seek repose; wish to achieve a level of serenity.

She sings the words of Shankara, transposes them to the present. *Sura mandira taru moolanivasaha, shayya bhootalam ajinam vasaha*...This voice, this voice that has felt, that knows what it describes, that is *bhava*, tells one with absolute certainty that grace exists. A balm that soothes, heals, this voice is a lap, a safe soft place where one can rest one's head, forget dark sorrow. Pure, shining, it is imbued with a beauty that adorns the gods, gives them their splendour, their compassion, and leads us to their hiding place, at the very heart of our hearts.

Punarapi jananam punarapi maranam punarapi janani jatthare shayanam...

Yet again birth, Death even again,
Again, yet again repose in a mother's womb...

This voice is known by two letters, her initials. The first, the place where she was born. The second, her mother's name: M.S.

Kastvam ko'ham kuta ayatah, ka me janani ko me tatah
iti paribhavaya sarvam asaram visvam tyaktva svapnavicaram

Truly, who are you? For that matter, who am I?
Where have we come from?
Who is my mother and who indeed
my father?
Let go of this essence-less dream-like world,
reflect instead
upon these questions.

~

Three days later, we visit Sangeeta at her house. I have scanned the area for danger and sensing no threat, I leave Sanju by the bookshelf while I talk to her.

'*Maa,*' he comes to me crying, his hand over his eye.

What? He has cut himself on the eyelid. The wound is like a small incision. My friend's mother clasps him to her bosom, blows warm air on her starched sari and rubs the wound vigorously. It is purple now, worse. I leave, drive to the hospital.

How? There was an edge to a table, he says, hidden under the cloth. It was eye-level. He banged into it.

In the emergency room, now familiar, a junior doctor attends to us and is nonplussed when Sanju asks for Dr. Rangarajan with a poise beyond his years. There is not a window in sight, a window that would let in the normality of sunshine, afford a view of trees and birds in a blue sky. Instead, there is artificial light and the gloom of mortality in the corners it does not reach.

The plastic surgeon arrives, sees Sanju and says to me, 'You're back so soon? I told you it would take a week to heal.' He shakes his head when he sees the wound. We are lucky. A millimetre elsewhere and his sight would have been damaged. It will heal on its own.

Through a doorway, I see the untidy ends of a mop making wet arcs of disinfectant on the tiles. Hospital smell. Two men hold Sanju down while the nurse dresses the wound. He screams, resenting the indignity of being subdued. It is a strain to understand the prescription; the handwriting and the doses. I pay the bill carrying Sanju on my hip.

'Ice cream?' he asks.

In the car, I slump, drained of the strength that had got me this far. I follow the car ahead of me blindly, not focussed on anything. The tail lights are blurred. A policeman waves me to a halt. 'Red light,' he says.

Where are the signals? It takes me a second to locate them. I am ashamed of the tears. I gesture to Sanju and say, 'I am taking him home from the hospital.' The man looks at my child, the gauze like a pirate's patch over his left eye, and is kind. He lets me go.

Actually, I am not in any condition to drive.

~

A cyclone skulks at sea, a compressed whorl of energy waiting for the right time to approach. At night the wind tears through the city, uprooting old venerable trees that have the temerity to stand upright in its path. The next morning, those huge trees look like toys flung by a bad-tempered giant, broken in play. Huts have collapsed, hoardings crumpled like paper, fishermen are lost at sea, and water maroons the residents of low-lying areas near the River Adyar.

In our garden, the jasmine creeper has been torn away from its support, it lies on the ground, folded upon itself. Everywhere leaves and branches lie broadcast. Rain pours incessantly from a sky grizzled with clouds. It is gloriously cool.

There is no school today. I dread what the advancing hours will bring.

How far I have come from the time when I welcomed surprises, sudden blessings, rain holidays…

~

Another day, another afternoon. I walk about the road in search of Thayee. She is not in the vacant property, nor is she under the neem. I try a passage that leads to a block of six flats. Two households there support her with the odd leftover. I find her seated on the flight of concrete stairs, curled weakly against the wall. The dim enclosure gives off a damp coolness.

Sensing my presence, she looks briefly at me before raising her eyes to the sky behind and above me. A blue flame glows in the centre of each eye. She quavers, 'Bhagavaane, you have protected me. I was wondering what to do, they have all gone out and I have nothing to eat.' Looking again at me, she says, 'Deivame, you are divinity personified.' She joins her hands in namaskaaram above her head and registers her praise, 'Kadavale. Kadavale.'

Disconcerted, made self-conscious, I ask where her vessel is. It is with all her other things. She wanders off to fetch it and I follow, not wanting her to walk back the entire way.

The single white cloth that she wraps loosely around herself reaches down only to her calves. The muscles of the calves are taut, flat as the rest of her sunburnt leg. Her arms and most of her back are bare; after the fashion of her village, she wears no blouse. Body inclined forward, knees slightly bent, she walks with a long stick held in her right hand, the road stretching ahead of her. I am reminded of the man who dressed himself in her image; who found in the homespun cloth such as Thayee wears, the way to freedom for an entire nation.

The uniformed watchman observes us. It is strange to see him at this time; usually he works the night shift. Beside him a servant woman squatting in the shade stares first at Thayee and then at me. There is disapproval on their faces, as also a certain incomprehension. Why should this old, useless woman benefit from the generosity of others?

152

'She does not even have the decency to wash that amma's vessel after taking the food,' says the woman severely, glowering at Thayee. The man snorts in agreement.

What business of hers is it? The gratuitous cruelty of her remark annoys me—I have taken a dislike to her.

A fly settles on the food, a quivering spot on the cool, milky surface; I wave it away and hold my hand like a shield over the plate.

Inside the compound, Thayee hunts under some soggy newspapers for her vessel. The bucket is misplaced as well. She locates it finally inside a cardboard carton. A crow lands on the ground, hopping closer in readiness. Another crow arrives, this one wholly black, beady eyes shining.

She rinses the dish with some brownish water from a plastic Pepsi bottle and holds it steady. The self in me that watches, the self that is aloof, distant, that self observes my hand sliding the food into the vessel and reminds me firmly that it is not 'I' who is giving it to her.

'Kadavale, Bhagavaane.'

I am not thorough enough: a few grains of rice remain and she wipes them off my plate with her fingertips.

'I don't have clean water here,' she says as I turn to leave, 'or I'd wash the plate.'

'I know,' I walk away, treading on my shadow. It moves like a black carpet unfolding ahead of me on the dusty road made golden with light. A pye-dog hovers nearby. The last traces of curd-rice are drying to tightness on my fingers, I must wash my hands. I pass the watchman and the woman. Two pairs of eyes sear my back with their idle, laser-like gaze until I reach home.

~

I find an old book of mine, its spine exposed, bands of thread holding the pages together. The cover separated itself a long time ago and when I pull it out of the shelf, the mottled first page reveals itself without modesty, immediate to the eye.

I had first read the book as an adolescent, very curious about childbirth — that distant certainty. Held by her description of it, I never forgot her use of the word *sliding*.

Now I can place my experience beside hers. My son never slid along my thigh like hers did, he shot out from within me and they placed him temporarily in a cradle nearby, separate, healthy, whole.

I start to read My Story again, but as I begin to follow her into the cool, dark spaces of Nalapat House, Sanju, son, tyrant, infant-ruler of my life flings himself across the bed and onto the book, demanding a bedtime story before going to sleep.

~

We visit Roshan Aunty in the hospital. She had always taken such trouble over her appearance that it is a shock to see her huddled in the bed. Mouth pursed without the dentures, her face crumpled. Her hair has grown, an inch of grey near the scalp, black from there onwards. The fight has gone out of her. She holds my arm with one hand and signals to a relative with the other to look in her bag for sweets to give Sanju.

Her hand is icy cold.

It is only on seeing her this vulnerable, shrunk inside the coarse, sack-like hospital gown, that one realises the tremendous effort she made all these years, this brave, feisty and devoted mother.

Sweety sits in a chair, swinging his legs.

The buttons on his shirt have been wrongly aligned: one flap hangs longer than the other, the collar awry.

~

It all happened because of a mango. Actually, two pairs of mangoes, one of this earth, the other celestial.

Punitavati hears a quaver outside, the call of a wandering mendicant, *'Bhavati bhiksham dehi...'* It is the traditional request for alms.

She is behind today, forgot herself at puja, and is yet to finish cooking. She can feel pin pricks in her hands, indecision, distress. What is she to do? Either way, she might shame herself, her family. She cannot send him away without alms, she cannot insult him with too meagre an offering. Before he can say those words again, she runs to the door.

She welcomes the stranger in, seats him, places a banana leaf before him. Troubled, she serves him silently, offers him all the rice she has cooked and curds to go with it. It is an incomplete meal. What else can she give him? Anxiety blanks her mind, wipes it of all thought. She could cry. He eats hungrily. What if he is expecting something more? The rice is finished.

She goes into the dim, barely lit kitchen, sits near the fire, elbow on knee, hand supporting her head. She could ask him to wait until she finishes cooking, but he has already begun eating.

Oh, she had almost forgotten. Relieved, she pats her forehead free of sweat, tucks her *pallu* in at her waist.

In a basket by the pile of wood, there are two mangoes. Her husband had them sent over that morning. He will be arriving soon for lunch. They are perfect, ripe. She walks back to her guest, overcome by the strange feeling that she has known him forever. Smiling now, she offers them graciously, with respect.

The guest is no ordinary being. He knows everything running through her mind. He eats one, declares Himself full. Before leaving, He raises His hand in blessing, grace brimming in His eyes, the third hidden under lines of ash on His forehead. He walks away, *danda*, *kamandalu* in hand.

She runs back to the kitchen, cooks rice once again, prepares vegetables, and is thankful that the pot of curds is half-full. When her husband reaches home, she has made a feast for him. She feeds him lovingly, giving him the mango towards the end of the meal. It is delicious. He asks for the other one. What is she to do now? Refuse her husband what she served a guest? She moves towards the kitchen as though to fetch the fruit.

Things press black upon her. Wringing her hands, she lifts her heart in prayer. *Help me. What am I to do?*

She has prayed to Him ever since she was a child. He who wears a serpent around His neck, runs to Him as she would her father. She separates her palms, discovers a beautiful mango with a flawless, golden skin. There is no time to assimilate the extraordinary; she rushes to serve her husband.

'Heavenly!' he exclaims. The taste of the second mango is so vastly superior, he asks her where she got it from. Hesitantly, fearing mistrust, she narrates the events of the morning.

'Really! Let's see if you can give me another.'

Tested the third time that day, once again she speaks from the heart to her Lord, asks for help, prays that her words be not proven false. Once again, it is given, gold weighing on her palm. He reaches for it.

The minute it leaves her hand, it disappears, her husband closing his fist on air. Astounded, he sees before him the true nature of his wife, finds himself unworthy of a goddess. She, child-like in her innocence, is unaware of her great virtue, her true quality. How can he touch her, knowing this? He chooses an auspicious day to leave home, says he is going away on a long voyage, in search of more wealth.

Each rising day, Punitavati awaits him with growing anxiety. What did she do that was so wrong, she wonders. Unknowingly, unintentionally, was she disrespectful to him in some way? Her mind shrinks from such a thought. Is he angry with her? Tears fill her eyes. If she could find one instance of having been remiss, it would be punishment enough. She finds nothing. Yet, she is convinced that she has somehow fallen from her ideal of being a pious, noble wife, amenable to the wishes of her husband, generous in giving alms.

In the evenings, she keeps replenishing the earthen lamps with oil, running from one to the other, lest the flame falter, expire and he not be able to find his way home.

Her father, a rich merchant in that port by the sea, enquires everywhere, hoping for news of Parama daathan, his son-in-law. Ships arrive and depart from busy Karaikkal, travellers wander all over the place. Did he arrive on one of those huge ships?

He grieves on seeing his beloved daughter unhappy, she from whom he could not bear to be separated, she for whom he found a bridegroom who would live in the same city.

Time passes.

One day, his men run to him excitedly. His son-in-law is well, alive, and settled in another kingdom. He fills their hands with coins, gems, reward for news both good and vital.

Punitavati is dressed like a bride. She wears silk and perfumes, is adorned with expensive jewellery and beautiful jasmine flowers are woven into her hair. Borne in a palanquin, she is taken on a journey to that other town. Her relatives escort her towards the place where he lives.

Parama daathan knew himself too well.

In the intervening time, he built wealth elsewhere, acquired a new wife, and from her, a child. He never thought that his past would travel to meet him, so many years later. He advances to where she is, seated in a grove. She stands up on seeing her husband.

Three human forms fall at her tender feet. He speaks of Punitavati as a goddess. Tells her shocked relatives that they do not know who she truly is. He can worship her, adore her from afar, but cannot be a husband to her. He draws his daughter forward, addresses Punitavati.

When the time came to name his infant, he paid tribute to her, he says, gave her the name of the purest soul he knows, Punitavati.

Silk ripped from her body, gold *thali* stripped away, silver *mettis* cracked. In a brutal instant, her bangles have been smashed, vermilion wiped off her face, widowhood thrust on her. Worse, death—a child named after her while she is still alive. Her husband's daughter, her daughter, a child she might have nourished in her womb. In that instant, she turns away from the world of mirage, its pretence, its specious allure.

Take away this beauty, take away this flesh, take away this yearning, take away ignorance. I have no use for it. I bore beauty of form, loveliness of visage for the sake of my husband. Make of me ghost, ghoul, no, departed soul. Yes, a pey, *a departed soul. May I always have my mind fixed on You.*

She retreats from him, moves towards the true beloved. He of matted hair, He who wears the silver sparkling ashes of burnt corpses, He with the sun, moon and fire for eyes.

He beams, grants her this singular, terrible wish. Fat melts away, flesh shrinks, skin wrinkles, adjusts itself to the thin reality of bone bereft of muscle. Her clothes disappear; there is nothing to hide. She wears the sky.

Breasts lose shape, shrivel, hair flames red. Her womb contracts, hip bones rise like hills over the flat floor of her belly. Veins creep varicose over her body. Thighs become thin, like sticks.

Her face is skull covered with a parchment of skin, the hollows under the cheek pronounced. Tear ducts close; henceforth, she will shed only tears of bliss. She exults in her skeletal figure, is free, free, light as air. Her eyes dance.

She knows that no sooner was she born, no sooner had she acquired words, than the great love she had for him impelled her relentlessly to attain His feet. That tremendous love within her that might have flowed in tributaries, *sringara* to her husband, *vatsalya* to her child, *daya-dana* to the wandering mendicant, she channels into a single potent force, reversing its flow towards the high, single source: *Bhakti*.

For her, no more the pleasant, no more the sensuous. No more comfort, no more ease. In the destruction that precedes creation, there is only Shiva, the auspicious.

She hugs the form of death, embraces the terrible, sings of it. Her poetry describes the dance of destruction, the hand that holds fire. He, blue of throat, stands by the blazing funeral pyre, rooting through charred sticks, charred bone. He, of long, streaming hair, stamps heavily on ignorance. He, wearing exquisite anklets on his feet, calls the world into being through the vibrations of sound.

She roams wild forests, inhabits cremation grounds. The austere is natural to her. She rests under the tamarind, the vaakai, the vilvam, the peepul. Broad, outstretched branches are like so many arms appealing to her Lord in the sky.

She sleeps in the open.

She exults at the sight of banyan trees, their immense trunks, the feel of the bark, the adventitious roots that look like the great pillars of a temple, the fickle breeze playing with her as with a ripple of heart-shaped leaves.

A shower of gold, the laburnum, a pendant cluster of blossoms, held separate by thin stems attached to a central stalk. Where she sees the abundant fall of yellow kondrai flowers, she sees Shiva, his luxuriant hair adorned in plenty.

Absentmindedly, she plucks a leaf or picks up a sour fruit, nibbling on it for food. She likes the delicate taste of the tip of the banyan root.

Her eyes feast on things she has never seen. There is a tree that bears beautiful deep blue flowers, whose name she does not know. A friendly spirit whispers its name to her, 'Kaaya maram...'

For company, she has an assortment of weird beings who cause her no trouble. A ghost who devours the flesh of dead bodies and perches blithely on a tree. Ghouls squealing, shouting, clapping their hands, shrieking through the night. They quarrel with one another, use their fists.

There is a female wraith who wears a garland of skulls and bones bleached white by the sun. She bears young ones called Kali, like her, teaches them for a while their hereditary trade, the skill of sucking flesh from cadavers. Capricious, she feeds them milk and then disappears, abandoning them. These young ones wake, search frantically for their mother in that desolate place.

There are shadowy creatures with fiery, glinting eyes, long nails, pointed teeth that pull half-burnt, decaying corpses out of the fire for a meal.

There are ferocious birds of prey, sly jackals, hungry fox. The shudugaattu malli blooms pink-purple amongst thorny, leafless plants on the outskirts of the burning ground. At night, the pods of the vaakai burst, the seeds dispersing with a loud, cracking sound.

Wandering transparent to all of them, she rejoices in this other dimension of truth, the ravenous, throbbing rhythm of it.

She knows with absolute certainty that He exists, can feel His presence everywhere and yet has never seen Him, a perplexing truth. When will He reveal Himself to her? She makes a pilgrimage.

Riding the winds, the clouds, she floats spirit-like over cities, arid lands, lakes, snow-laden mountain ranges. She reaches the foot of Kailash. The Sweet One who abides in her heart dwells there. His sacred home, she cannot sully it with her feet.

She bows in obeisance, head bent, her hands flat on the ground, body folded over the knees. Carefully, she tips her weight, stops mid-somersault, unwinds her body vertically. Legs forked, swaying, it takes her a while to accustom herself to a different balance. She walks on her hands, climbs the mountain with speed, intent on seeing Him.

At the peak, when she beholds His beautiful, lotus-like feet adorned with anklets, a mellifluent bell tied slightly higher, her head is already level with them.

Parvati sees that strange apparition, enquires of Shiva who it is. He tells her that she is one who has remarkable, unswerving love for Him. A love located within a human heart, caged within the confines of bone and yet as vast as the boundless universe, Shiva Himself.

Once, she welcomed Him into her home, fed Him with care, trepidation in her heart. It is His turn to receive, be host. He goes forward, welcomes her with respect, with great affection. He, the *swayambhu*, addresses her with a single word:

'*Ammaiye!*'

She regards her father, feet first.

Shiva grants her a boon—sprung free of the tumultuous ocean of birth, death, birth repeated, she will witness every dance of His from the vantage of His moving feet.

She makes her way back south to an area forested with the spreading banyan, in great anticipation. The sleepy settlement of Thiruvalangadu will be made holy, the place where Shiva will dance. She is witness to it.

A sculptor of the Chola period portrays her in bronze, cymbals in hand, face rapt, a single thought running electric through her emaciated being: Shiva. One of the few women among sixty-three exalted devotees of Shiva, she is adored as

Karaikkal Ammaiyaar, the pey who roamed the forests of Thiruvalangadu sometime in the 6th century BC.

Her poetry is unique in many ways.

~

That divinity abiding in every being in the form of compassion,
I bow my head before Her, again and again and again
and yet again.

That divinity abiding in every being in the form of good fortune,
I bow my head to Her, again and again and again
and yet again.

It is a thought that recurs, the pressure charring my mind until it crumbles in a black powdery mass. I want out. And yet, if I am not there, who will look after him? The very thing that pushes one to a precipice is that which saves. In ten minutes, I must feed him his lunch.

Craving peace, I close my eyes and in the blankness see myself dead. A lifeless body floating on the supportive, flowing waters of the Ganga, lying on a pallet, covered with flowers. Open to sky, bobbing past the rising steps of the *ghats*. Peace.

And yet, the mind hovering, watching this procession, for it can only imagine this scene, never witness it yoked to the body, protests. *Where is he?* I accommodate him here as well. Place him by my side, watch over him as my body floats towards tranquillity.

'What is worn out, broken, loosened, powerless, disturbed, crushed, or destroyed, consider that a new beginning' —Sage Vashishtha speaks to me, describes my present state of mind, offers sustenance with his words written more than a score of centuries ago.

~

I leave Sanju at the door of his class and return to the car.

I see a father stroll by, holding his daughter's hand. He is dressed for work, black polished shoes, formal shirt and a tie. They are laughing. He carries her satchel and lunch bag in the other hand. Tears prick my eyes. Why has that simple pleasure been denied to my child?

What is it that makes things happen? Why do things happen when they do? I have not been able to gift him the childhood I had, secure in the love of both parents. How can I give him something that is not mine to give—a father's love?

I am his bodyguard. I do not leave him even for a second for fear that he will somehow hurt himself. I used to think I was a lioness when it came to protecting him, until I saw the photograph of a mother snake, her body coiled around the eggs, her hood poised to strike. I am like that mother snake.

And yet, despite all my care, accidents happen.

A thought comes to me, brings great comfort: *Ishvara* gathers us in his lap when we sleep. What if…

The lamps are lit, a single flame in each lamp, intense, steady. Incense spirals around freshly plucked flowers.

I close my eyes and concentrate on the space between my brows.

I place Sanju on His lap, on the left side, the softer, maternal half of Him and pray that Sanju remain in His lap when he is awake as well as asleep.

The next day, at puja, I see that Sanju cannot sit passively in His lap. It is against his nature. He does not let Him talk, keeps interrupting Him, holds His face with both his palms and turns it towards himself. He asks Him why

165

He has an extra eye, rubs the blue paint on His neck. He climbs up to His shoulder, plays with the snake, pulling it by its tail. Sanju then finds a loop of bone. He tugs at it and He winces.

Tiring of that after a while, Sanju climbs higher, from where he can hear the sound of rushing water. There is ash all over him. Maa *will scold him for dirtying his clothes*. He comes upon a bright, crescent-shaped toy held in place by brownish curls. It's a slide. He sails down its inner curve for a while before the sound of water draws him higher, higher.

A *gana* is deputed to keep track of him.

He enters a big river, splashes about with great joy, bathes in its pure waters. Tired, he rides the waterfall, tumbling all the way down to His lap, where he sleeps a happy, dreamless sleep.

'Don't complain to me,' I tell Him. 'I told you he is not easy to manage. At least You have all the *ganas* for help.'

Henceforth, Sanju will step into the outside protected by the armour of a mother's prayer.

~

Thayee has accumulated so many things that there is no room for her under the sunshade. The brown peaks of the cardboard boxes stretch all the way across the front door. Plastic bags of all kinds and sizes lie about, some empty, some holding more bags within them. Near the steps leading to the roof, a length of hosepipe lies coiled upon itself. On the window sill, there are two brown medicine bottles and a comb. One cannot see her from the road, as was possible earlier when she sat near the door.

She has made herself a bed near the wall. She has acquired a silvery grey plastic mat that must have been used as some sort of covering and has placed a bundle of cloth on it, at the head. As far as the eye can see, every inch of vacant land has been occupied by some possession of hers, by things that are broken, empty, used, useless, torn, redundant. A pair of leather shoes tramples a tuft of wild grass. The left shoe is in good condition, the right has a hole at the toe.

Near the lumpy pillow, on the ground are at least fifteen hibiscus flowers, all red, of both the single and double variety. In that place, where everything speaks of depletion and waste, where things have faded or become filthy, lost the colour they once owned, where even the green of the trees is overladen with dust, in that sad place this deep glowing colour is the colour of life itself.

'Thayee, why do you bandage them to your forehead?'
'What?'
Having begun, I persevere. 'These flowers, why do you…'
'They flow to the eyes…cool water…'
I cannot understand what she is saying. The quaver and the dialect are difficult to cut through. When I ask again, she gets irritated and glares at me. I give up.

Outside, the day watchman and Malar, the maid who works in Fatima's house, stand face-to-face, gossiping. I ask them instead. They are amused.

'It's cooling,' says the watchman, with a wide grin. 'She thinks it will heal her eye.' Malar grins as well. 'Just like a paste of the hibiscus leaves is good for the hair.'

'If she can't see, why doesn't she consult a doctor,' says Malar, unconcernedly.

'It takes money,' murmurs the watchman, very impressive in his khaki uniform with the stiff epaulettes and gleaming brass buttons.

'Nothing like that. There are so many free clinics for the poor,' insists Malar, tilting her head at him, 'why can't she go there?'

'And how will she get there?' he smiles, his teeth in sparkling contrast with the black of his moustache.

Malar drops the argument and smiles instead, in agreement. *How does it matter after all, the crone is half-mad anyway. The watchman is more interesting!* She looks at the plate I am carrying and I can see the amusement extending to include me as well: good-hearted but naïve amma—*why is she wasting food on a wretch who is better off dead?*

~

The driver has come in later than usual and has the company of his friend, the day watchman, while he cleans the car. I drive past them and stop in front of the gate, preparing to open it.

Unexpectedly, the driver hurries across and opens the gate for me. All the impressions, gathered randomly through the years, come together now. He was punctual, regular, as far as I can tell, even in the monsoons, and his manner towards his employers was courteous in an old-fashioned way. When Fatima and her mother sat in the car, he bore them away solemnly, as though something precious and extremely fragile was in his charge. I am curious to know how he lost his job but hesitate, uncertain as to where exactly in his mind he will draw the fine line between idle curiosity and familiarity. Besides, I have never spoken to him before.

168

I decide to ask.

'Got a job yet?'

'*No!*,' he says, rotating his wrist, his fingers spread apart in a gesture conveying nothingness. '*Abhi* neutral *me hein.*' He grins, pleased with his pun. There is a molar missing and somehow this makes him look boyish in the brief instant that his teeth are revealed.

In the distance, near Palani's house, a woman struggles with the piston of a pump, bringing all her weight to bear on its passage downwards. The sound it produces has an asymmetrical rhythm to it, a long protesting sigh as it works the water up and through the spout and then a short metallic squeak as it flies easily, unhindered, back to its natural position.

I look at him again. 'What happened?'

'I needed money,' he replies, 'I asked them for a loan and they wouldn't give it. So I quit.'

'But now you'll need it all the more,' I say but he is not listening to me. He is thinking something through, his eyes locked on the thought. I worry that he is going to ask me for a job. He emerges from his debate with himself, suddenly impatient, and retreats to the extreme side of the driveway to let me pass.

I drive in and he is lost from sight in the rear-view mirror as he closes the gate for me.

'*Jaako aata...*' he takes leave of me in a despondent voice, fidgeting with the latch on the gate.

~

Roshan Aunty died a week ago.

Sweety, heir to everything his parents possessed, was left in the care of his uncle. One morning, he left their house,

169

barefoot, searching for his mother. He reached a home nearby where she used to take him frequently, where he felt loved, and sought her there. He rambled through the rooms, calling out for her, his eyes scanning the ceiling. His guardian arrived an hour later.

Sweety has been on tranquillisers since.

~

Two weeks ago, a boil had developed on Sanju's gums. The dentist said the infection was bad and that the front tooth would have to be extracted. Already, the area between the two front teeth has corroded.

'Baby-bottle syndrome,' said the dentist, by way of explanation.

It took a barrage of questions, some repeated, some rephrased, to understand that all those nights when I had spilled powder into a bottle, made milk for him around two in the night, groping my way through sleep and exhaustion, I had been damaging his teeth. The sugar remained in his mouth, delighting bacteria, every night for two years, while I thought I was feeding a hungry toddler.

So, he has a gap in his teeth prematurely.

'You can eat a peanut without opening your mouth,' I tease him, hiding dismay.

All of a sudden, Sanju says, 'I have another boil.'

It is on the side this time. I run my finger over it and hurry to the clinic. The x-ray reveals another bad infection, a lot of pus. So on Saturday they will extract another tooth, a premolar.

He sits in the now familiar dentist's chair, excited by the tray of instruments and the exotic attention of three masked adults. He is brave, he has aplomb. Trusting me, he submits to all of this. I shall never complain about him again.

He makes a great show of gargling when asked to. The minute he can remove the bib and get off the chair, he discovers the raising mechanism and begins to raise and lower the chair.

It has taken fifteen days for the insidious germs to win a war in his mouth. Simple math, if he develops one boil a month, in a year all his teeth will be gone! I brush his teeth twice a day, don't give him many sweets; nothing makes sense. Through the gloom, the thought that troubles—it must be my fault. These are milk teeth, I remind myself and am thankful to God for the second chance.

I treat him to an ice cream as soon as we leave the place.

~

Sanju and Ram weave all over the road on their cycles. I stand to one side, watching.

The flocks of birds that appear in the sky move swiftly, hurrying past the tired sun. They fly in one direction, north, and my eyes travel with them, tracing a line that began in a patch of clear blue sky on the left and disappears somewhere above the spiky head of a coconut tree. The local crows are an exception, content as they are with the lower atmosphere, the scraps of food from dustbins and a circular migration among the garden trees.

Thayee is over at the other end, facing me. She achieves the length between us with slow effort, staff in one hand, a plastic cup in the other.

A car turns round the corner, and a moped starts up with a rapid gunfire of sound, carrying blithely that burden of noise as it moves. They disrupt the picture like a pebble scattering water; the children dissolve and regroup on the sides in a madness of rippling limbs and excitement. I cannot locate Sanju along the bank of safety. The small bodies surge forward impatiently, almost touching the moving vehicles, covering space given up temporarily. I search the confusion of colours, and it is only when I see a green T-shirt and beige shorts resolved happily on a cycle, that the tension recedes.

When Thayee reaches me, she stops walking and sinks down on the road to rest.

'Where did you go?'

She points to the plastic cup with a grimy finger, 'There's an amma there, in the small house near the main road. She gives me coffee in the evenings, like you do in the mornings.'

After a while she says, 'I am not able to eat much these days. I have saved some of the rice you gave me for the night. What is the point of living like this? The son I gave birth to, my own son, doesn't even acknowledge me.'

'How many children do you have, Thayee?'

She watches my lips move, but cannot read the shape of the syllables. She stands up and moves closer to me.

I dance my question for her, 'How many,' a closed fist with the thumb pointing upwards, 'children?' palms supporting the small head and bottom of a baby.

She holds up four fingers. Then, understanding my intent, she says, 'One girl lives in Velachery. Her husband does not have any work. He roams around collecting rubbish and manages somehow. The second one earns twenty rupees a day. That is not enough for him to feed his wife and himself. He wants me to live with him. She will keep me well but they are struggling themselves. This one is the worst,' she waves her hand in the direction of the buffaloes. 'His wife would kill me if she could.'

A yellowish fluid is oozing out of her left eye. It has reached the cheek bone where it rests momentarily.

'You yourself saw how he behaved... I was the one who found that bit of land all those years ago, but he won't even let my shadow cross the door. When I went to use the toilet there, he beat me so badly, blood came pouring out of my eye. Can't hear anything, now I cannot see. And the one who came empty-handed, not an ounce of gold on her, look at her, she lacks for nothing today!' She does not seem to expect an answer from me.

'It's getting dark. Call out to your son, amma. Take him home.'

Only later do I realise that in my anxiety to understand her, to follow what she was saying in the unfamiliar dialect, I had forgotten to ask her about her fourth child.

~

The last time I danced on stage, something unusual had happened. And because it had never happened before, it was unnerving as well. Eyes closed, I enter the memory of that particular performance, in Madras at the Academy:

A lone figure on stage. To my right, a row of seated musicians. In front, beyond the over-arching glare of light, a semicircle of darkness hiding the audience. The stage is large and difficult to cover in movement. Centre-stage was marked with a strip of white tape but it *felt* disconcertingly off-centre. I think I had worn my maroon costume with a green border that day, draped like a sari.

The relief of finishing the *varnam*, body hot, heart beating madly, costume wet with sweat. Applause. Lights being dimmed and the musicians finishing the count with the final tap on the *mridangam*. I had made one mistake, but there was no time to think about it. Ahead, three pieces expanding on *abhinaya* before the *tillana* at the end.

Relaxed, comfortable now with the variable elements of that place: the slippery wooden floor, lighting, the exits from the stage. On to the *ashtapadi Raase harimiha*, where Radha, separated from Krishna, remembers every little detail of his appearance. His quivering lips pressed against the flute, bringing forth the sweetest of sounds. His earrings, the way they brush his cheeks, from side to side as he moves. The peacock feather with the half-moon centre, decorating his long hair. It is a difficult piece to perform; these details must be presented as part of her longing, not as a standard description of Krishna. After Sir taught me the meaning, I spent hours thinking about the poem, finding ways to make my interpretation different, unique.

It is a beautiful *ashtapadi*, such a poignant mix of *viraha*, separation and *adhbuta*, wonder and admiration. Radha remembers their love-play, their meeting beneath the giant kadamba tree and the thought of his dallying with other *gopi*s seems a mockery of those times they spent together. He is the only one who is right for her, just as she knows for certain, that she is the only one right for him. Is ridicule implicit in his neglect of her?

Somewhere in the middle of the slow tempo of the piece, in Bageshree, there is a lull where she is pensive, her eyes closed. Charu, the singer that day, was sublime. She sang with *bhava*. I held the pose, hands holding Krishna's flute but the face and body language that of a yearning Radha, knowing it would be a while before the next word would be sung, marking a shift. The brain busy, absorbed, directing every muscle—face, hands, legs. A silent voice admonishing my right elbow: up, up, no slack, and my knees: bend, sink lower, forget the discomfort.

Suddenly, I found a place for myself, on that stage, in front of so many people, that was mine alone. I was lost, far away. Perfect, perfected, in time and yet out of it, aware of my limbs held in position, but lost to everything else. I had slipped out of myself, peace, great peace, a golden nothingness... And then, the moment ended with the word being sung, the music flowed on and I returned to myself, relieved that I had not missed a beat, terrified that I might have.

I never told anyone about it. What if they had laughed?

How I long to return to that immense, calm place again.

~

'Shiva *Bhagavaan* carries the moon in his hair?'

'Yes, my precious.' I look up and see a tiny bow of silver. 'Look there! When the moon looks like that, it is called a crescent moon. That's the moon He wears.' We are on the roof where I convoke celestial bodies to help me feed him dinner: Moon, stars, clouds, constellations, planes, and once, a marvellous rainbow. He surveys infinity and beholds the ornament suspended in the black sky of Shiva's hair.

'He's there right now?'

I caress his cheek. Sweet.

'Whenever you see the moon, He's there with you.'

~

That divinity abiding in every being in the form of movement,
I bow my head before Her, again and again and again
and yet again.

That divinity abiding in every being in the form of memory,
I bow my head before Her, again and again and again
and yet again.

It is a month of early prayer, of waking before dawn. A month favoured over others, for, of all the months, Krishna says he is *Margazhi*. In the chill of darkness, Thayee's granddaughter spends an hour on her haunches. A steady, concentrated trickle of rice flour from her hand leaves elaborate patterns on the ground. The half-light of dawn reveals a flowery carpet flung around white, perfectly rounded dewdrops.

Dance and music overwhelm Madras: The Season, as it is called. The schedule at many homes is altered while connoisseurs attend show after show, dressed in their finest. In an atmosphere of celebration almost, old acquaintances meet, gossip, part and meet again at another auditorium. Newspapers carry the names of dancers and the places where they will perform, an advertisement of who has the most number of shows. When people ask me, 'Are you performing anywhere?' I shake my head. I shall attend my guru's performance, dance vicariously through him.

The skin rejoices at the feel of silk; there is a nip in the air. The watchman makes a bonfire at night, and is pleased with its novelty, its cheering warmth. He also wears a masklike cap that adds mystery to his job. It covers his ears, mouth, cheeks, leaving a square opening for his eyes. The back of his head is covered entirely.

Some nights, Thayee will linger near the glowing embers of the dying fire, the watchman fast asleep on a chair.

She does not sleep much these days. I see her from the window, weaving her way from house to house, in the depths of the night. Her back is bare save for a diagonal of cloth. *She should wear something thicker, otherwise she will fall sick. It is cold at night now.* At a time when everyone chooses a degree of warmth in their clothing, Thayee walks about with rags wrapped around her. It is futile to give her a rug or a thicker sari. Amma gave her a blanket once. She sold it; slept the night exposed.

I think about the sameness of her life, its mundane repetitions and I see its parallels in my life. One day follows the other, routine, and yet one is unable to establish it in entirety, state with certainty that one will be faithful to it the next day.

~

Admiring the saris hanging in my cupboard, I settle on one: silk imbued with the shimmer of a peacock's neck, gold border. *When was the last time I wore it?* I leave Sanju behind with my parents and leave for the show. I savour the rich folds of the sari, the gorgeous play of colour, now blue, now green when I walk, spine erect.

Backstage, Sir is hidden within a circle of adoring students. I see familiar faces, exchange smiles, greetings as I make my way towards him. His costume is blue with a yellow cloth draped around the waist. He is withdrawn, has already entered the mental space created in the process of make-up and costume. There is the elongated mark of divinity on his forehead, made of sandalwood paste. A number of gold ornaments draw the eye to his otherwise bare arms and chest, simple jewellery appropriate to the male dancer. Where lesser dancers are submerged by costume and make-up, he assumes them with poise. The rouge and lipstick that look pronounced now, will fade under the lights. I bend and touch his feet, and when others surge towards him, I leave to find a place in the darkened auditorium; enter home.

I hold my breath, feel a thrill in the pit of my stomach. He is to perform a piece that he does to perfection, one of my favourites from the *Krishna-karnamritam*.

Five musicians sit to the left, on the stage. A singer holding cymbals and three instrumentalists: the *mridangam*, flute and the violin. Behind them, the straight-backed majesty of the *tambura*.

A brief essay of the *raga* Mohanam. Notes swell from the flute, create a village, cows and the homes of milkmaids. The stage is gradually lit and Sir enters from the side, the skin of his upper body golden in the light, the blue silk flaring with each step. He is neither tall, nor short; just right for a dancer, with a muscular body not inclined to fat.

Centre-stage, a spotlight holds him within its beam while a smoky dimness surrounds him. A pair of naughty eyes peer around a door, search for temptation and brighten when they find it. The little boy, legendary for his pranks, pushes open the door of a simple cottage and sneaks in, seeking relief from the heat outside. The pot is hanging from the ceiling, out of his reach. The magic of dance, the eyes register a self-assured grown man on stage but see a mischievous little boy.

The lights grow stronger. He stands on his toes, then jumps, his hands outstretched, but he cannot even touch the pot. He places his index finger on his chin, thinking hard. Idea! Swiftly he pulls his flute from the waistband and hits the bottom of the pot with it. Buttermilk gushes out of the hole, and he cups his hands under the flow, not minding the fact that it runs down his arms, drips down his bent elbows. Glorious, cool, refreshing buttermilk. The last drop lapped up, he wipes his mouth with the back of his hand.

He looks around. Butter and sugar? Where does she keep that delicious mixture of butter and sugar, *navaneetam*? Suddenly, apprehensive of danger, he looks at the door and finding no one there, relaxes. Butter. What is that unusually tall jar over there, in that corner? The tinkle of bells as he first runs to it, a hush as he slows down and moves stealthily, the music held in abeyance.

Hundreds of bells on Sir's ankle lie still at his command as he places foot after tentative foot in search of butter. The cymbals that accompany each movement of the dancer, helping to create effect, fall silent as well.

The child leans against the length of the stone jar, peers in. Creamy butter, freshly churned, mmm...mmm..., his hands sink into sweet delight and he swallows great gulps of it. He is absorbed now, by the butter, the taste of it, the enormous quantity of the treasure he has found.

He does not hear the sound.

In a swift change of role, turning half a circle away from where he stood, Sir is now the milkmaid, the feminine essence captured in every little gesture of his. He walks with the swaying grace of a woman carrying heavy pots of milk on her head. She lifts them off her head, enters her home, sees the busy intruder, a smear of butter on the peacock feather in his hair. Faced with that charming sight, her heart melts faster than butter in heat. Feigning strictness, she draws attention to herself with a clap.

'Who are you, little boy?' The violin asks the question as the singer sings the words of the poem.

Shocked, he turns in a flash, teeters, his hands immersed in the jar. He tries to take them out, then thinks the better of it. Opening his eyes wide, 'The younger brother of Bala.' The flute replies on his behalf.

What a show of innocence!

She is dying to laugh, grab him and cuddle him, but she questions him further.

'Why are you here?'

Hands immobilised in the jar, Sir's eyes speak now, chase the flow of thought in little Krishna's mind. Is it possible she hasn't seen the pot with the hole in it? Is it just possible she has not noticed his proximity to the jar? He might just get away with it!

He embarks on a story. The raised eyebrows, troubled face, round eyes, and cherubic chin lifted at an angle, convey great honesty.

It was hot. He was on his way home to his mother Yashoda. But in the dazzle of sunlight, all the homes looked alike and he entered this one, mistaking it to be his home. He drops his eyes, looks sideways, out of the corner of his eye, wondering what the response will be. It just might work. He looks casually away, in the direction opposite the hanging pot.

181

What a darling, I think. No wonder he got away with theft after theft of butter! Who could be angry looking at that child there? Simultaneously, pride swells within me. That is my guru on stage. I learnt from *him*.

Hiding her smiles, the milkmaid demands an explanation, 'That may be likely, but why have you slipped your hand into the depths of the pot of butter?'

Krishna looks down at his hands. Amazement as he discovers them in the pot. Consternation. How did they ever get there? Why, he has butter all over him! He has to think of something fast. Aah. An explanation. Even greater innocence now, calculated to charm.

'Oh! I was searching for my calf. It was lost. I thought it was hiding in here. In a moment I shall leave.'

The scene has been danced in seconds, the *mudra* showing an unusually small cow, the size of a large fly wandering about on the streets of the village before miraculously flying into the jar of butter! Krishna solemnly peering into the jar, carefully moving aside folds of butter, terribly solicitous of the well-being of his calf. The imp! The rogue!

There is a sustained applause. Every single heart here has been touched. My hair stands on end.

I start to clap while looking around me — see beaming faces everywhere, blue jager diamonds afire on the elderly lady next to me. I hear appreciation in the applause, gratitude for having been taken away from care for a while.

Now returned to his self, Sir accepts the compliments with folded hands and a bow.

The tremendous power of art! A human being, alone on a stage, supported only by music, expressing the emotions of a character, creating a corresponding feeling in every person sitting in the audience. *Bhava*. What great audacity is required of a dancer, to actually attempt such a thing as create *rasa!* Many have failed in the endeavour.

The dance, ephemeral creation of visual poetry, has ended. The stage is empty. But in the minds of those who watched, an indelible impression has been left behind.

When I return home, I am faced with an enumeration of Sanju's misdeeds: he left the fridge open, he would not eat his dinner, he was rude, he this, he that.

The joy I have carried all the way home, drains from my heart, ebbs away. Dancing *vatsalya*—love for a child—is perhaps far easier than bringing up a child in real life.

Surely that is why, of all the different terms of honour, Shiva chose to call Punitavati *ammaiye*—Mother.

~

A girl crouches comfortably on the freshly prepared ground. Leaning forward, she draws a line that curves around a single dot, embracing and enclosing it. It is a flowing line, beginning randomly, but travelling many distances before ending at the point where it began. When the eye falls on it, however, one cannot tell the beginning or the end. It is self-contained, simultaneously a puzzle and its solution. A pattern, a symbol. Food for the ants, decoration for the gods.

The fronts of most houses display the talent of a single person, maid or mistress. Our Poongavanam, however, is disinterested. Her efforts are small, mostly straight lines, sticks set across each other. What she does is facile and quick, in an impatient gesture.

183

The girl is Thayee's granddaughter. Every morning and evening at the gates of the house where she works, she effaces a faded creation, dissolves it with water. She then drops white rice-flour on the clean road, describes continuity and perfection with fluid strokes.

In this month of *Margazhi* she surpasses herself. The more the number of dots, the more intricate her self-expression. The more the number of dots, the more difficult it is for the twisting, moving line to reach the end unbroken, without mishap. She stores countless sequences in her memory, recalls them by shape or the number of dots. Her idea of herself is defined by this ability.

The *kolam* spreads across the road, touches both ends. Today it is circular in shape and it levitates, spins like a disc of white gold above the tar.

She walks away from her art, lost in a silent world. Deaf, mute.

A while later, a dented Fiat car rolls past and carries away dots and evanescent curves on its tyre.

~

On some days, I dangle between hope and despair. I will never be able to find a space within which to retreat, dance. On others, I have a vision of a cupboard stacked with unpublished manuscripts, wrapped in brown paper that I will leave to Sanju. He might not read a single one of them.

As a distraction, I begin to arrange old papers—immature poems and stories written by me in a childish scrawl—in a drawer when I come upon a file. It contains all the newspaper reviews of my performances, the clippings stuck neatly on sheets of paper with the name of the publication and dates marked as well. I look at my pictures in them, recall the one sentence that thrilled me no end: 'She has the inner feeling for dance that makes all the difference.'

Thinking about it, I wonder what it means that, at a point in time, this was said about me. What weight does that sentence carry? What weight does the learning obtained from my guru with hard work, with persistence, carry? Who determines its value?

Something else occurs to me. It is a disturbing thought, a question with a simple, straightforward answer. I ask Appa, hoping there might be another answer.

'What will happen if I don't dance, or don't write. All these books in my head. What if I don't ever write them?'

He looks at me, calmly puffing on his pipe.

'It doesn't matter to the world in general. Right? Thousands of books have been written over the years that nobody reads anymore. I don't need to add to them. The world will go on. The same with dance. There are other dancers.'

He nods his head in agreement. He understands what I mean.

'So then?'

'You dance for your own happiness: *Swaantaha sukhaaya*.'

It's all in the mind, then. This thing that impels from within, I want to extinguish it, jump on it, crush it. Wrap my hand around it and pull it out by its pernicious roots.

At puja, I tell Him to withdraw my gifts from me, give them to someone else who can use them. I lay my ankle bells down at His feet, put aside the dreams of a book bearing my name on it. 'I submit,' I tell Him. 'I surrender to Your wishes. I accept that I may never dance, or that when I do, it will be when You desire, O Nataraja, Lord of Dance.'

'At your feet, give me a little space beside Karaikkal Ammaiyaar. Or maybe, a place beneath *her* feet. When I danced the story of her life, I recognised so much of myself in her.'

Saranagati, prappatti, atma-samarpanam, Ishvara-pranidhaana — different words leading to the same thing: surrender.

'Just look after my child, that's all I ask of You. You alone are his mother, his father, You are relative and friend as well, You are learning, You are wealth, You alone are everything, my Lord of Lords.'

~

All of a sudden, there is the shock of clear, empty space between the road and the house. There are ten or eleven labourers on the premises, resolute, focussed, each the master of one single skill. They have been at work for some hours now, wreaking the destruction that precedes the creation of the new. The cracked walls that enclosed the land, that defined the limits of possession to the very square-inch have been pulled down. The old house, mercilessly exposed, looks small, incapable of affording shelter to anyone.

Bicycles that were parked earlier in the morning beside the security of brick, stand between rubble and road, marking the boundary arbitrarily. Some have a tiny triangle fixed to the metal bar in front, part ornament, part accessory — a seat for a small child. The spokes glint in the sun.

It was inevitable — someone looking for land close to the main road would make an offer and the owners would convert their burden of property into cash.

A slender woman has set up a makeshift kitchen under the coconut tree. Soot blackens the lower half of a dented aluminium pot placed on bricks. She stokes the flames with a fan made of palmyra leaves.

Thayee sits beside the woman, not perturbed in the least by the noisy confusion manifest around her. Her things are still spread out the way they were the night before. Dust, fresh, white, released by the walls in defence, has come to rest upon them, masking them in a uniform manner. She stares dreamily into the distance where a man is fighting with the last recalcitrant bit of wall.

The morning after, there is again the sound of pounding, of an instrument being brought to bear repeatedly, to rhythm almost, on something solid. At first, it is an assault— direct, powerful blows by an invisible assailant on the ear. Gradually, it recedes to form a part of the background of noises that inform one of the time of the day. Sometime between the joyous shrieks of the birds gliding towards the river and the brass bell being rung at puja, the sounds cease.

The roof of the house has been broken down by the simple but powerful combination of primitive instruments and human will. Bare-chested men wielding giant hammers climb down from their respective locations on the building.

One corner of the house remains standing, the walls flanking the crease slope giddily down the hypotenuse to the ground. The windows, rendered useless, creak listlessly in the wind. The doors inside have been dismantled and stacked to one side.

The jagged hull of the house now holds within it the view of what lies beyond. The shaggy coconut trees at the back and an immense gulmohar tree spread against the darkening sky seem like a scene freshly but incompletely painted over an old, fading canvas of a house.

It takes the men two days to break the house. The inside of the damaged brick is surprisingly red as though all this time thick blood flowed through the cells of grey cement. The rubble is heaped onto a lorry and the doors and windows are removed from the site, revealing a clean stretch of moist, loose soil with a trench dug all around it.

The area has been mapped into squares and rectangles by strings tied to inch-high wooden pegs pushed into the soil. A child's plan of a make-believe home, almost. Here a bedroom, here the kitchen, here the room for the gods. The trees in front have been felled and transformed into firewood.

Material for construction has devoured a part of the road, turning it into a spacious workshop, open to sun and rain. There is a large pyramid of river sand and a smaller pyramid of sharp-edged, black stones in front of the plot. On the side, bricks are stored in a solid, impenetrable column, blocking the neighbour's view.

Planks lie on the verge, piled untidily. Goats tread these uneven shelves to savour crisp, forbidden shrubbery from the garden wall. Huge tin drums that once stored tar now hold water. These dented and rusty receptacles are grouped haphazardly on the land skirting the road.

The ends of a faded cotton sari have been knotted around a high branch of a tree. A baby sleeps in the centrefold of the improvised cradle, rocked by the breeze. Her mother is a labourer. She carries bricks balanced on her head, back perfectly straight, hands by her side. Periodically, she will lift the baby free of the folds of cloth, settle her against her malnourished self and drop her *pallu* over the suckling infant. Walking past, one sees a thin, calm woman, sari swathed loosely about her shoulders, resting against a tree.

Wooden poles have been propped against the trunk of a tree. Iron rods are cut to size on a makeshift work-bench set up on the road. There is just enough space left for a car to pass through.

Any surface purveys for Thayee a bed: on the bare wall of the doctor's house; on top of the heap of pliant sand; inside an auto-rickshaw; on the unsteady pile of planks; on a *thinnai*.

She particularly likes the area in front of the gate of our house. At night, the headlights of the car briefly illuminate a bundle, a line of bone, something covered with a dirty cloth. One has to be cautious while returning home, so as not to run over her.

~

We drive home from school. Sanju clutches his report card, trying to decipher it. 'A, A, A,' he says, happy that this mysterious, pleated thing is so easy to read. What he can't read are the teacher's remarks that serve as great reaffirmation: 'Highly energetic and restless.'

The sky is overcast. The light emanating from the sun is weak. It gives not the blessing of warmth. Sanju looks at the sun, sees an orb, half gold, half silver in a hazy sky and he points at it excitedly, saying 'Look Maa, a moon made of the sun!' I smile and look up at the sky; it seems odd to be able to stare at the sun, sans glare, sans dazzle. The holidays have begun.

What will I do the whole day with him? I am crazed already.

~

He has exhausted what the planet has to offer. He spurns puzzles, does not want to colour silly shapes, toys that yielded readily to his probing lie in pieces, and his ball is lost. He is not hungry. He flops against me, his limbs loose and heavy. I brought him into being, I must provide preparation. It is too hot to go outside.

A memory from childhood. It startles me. Such a long time has passed since I last recalled the moment. My parents are visiting close friends of theirs; a playwright and his wife. I am seven or eight years old, dressed in a pavadai. There is animated conversation, much laughter followed by a heavy meal. It is summer and the dry heat of Delhi makes the brick and cement house feel like an oven. The grown-ups decide to take a stroll—at least there is a cool, gentle breeze blowing outside. Appa lifts me up. I am drowsy; it is way past my bedtime, but I do not want to miss anything in this new city. I fight sleep.

Lying in the snug palanquin of Appa's arms, my head pillowed in the bend of his elbow, I see the faraway stars twinkle in the dark sky moving above me, and say, 'I'm bored.' It is a word I have recently learned.

Appa, taking me seriously as he always has, replies, 'You are too young to be bored, my dear,' his stately voice resonating from deep within the shirt against my cheek.

I read Sanju a story. On the wall in front of me, above the dining table, Yashoda leans towards Krishna, pointing to the sky. An old woman watches them. Her black veil has slipped to one side. They inhabit the fluid landscape of a Kangra miniature. The plump child sits on the floor, his eye following the trajectory of his mother's finger. A shallow basin of water has been placed in front of him. When he looks down, he will see the full moon captured within. I understand her, at this age, understand that she will grant him anything, anything that will hold his attention, prevent ennui from seizing him.

I give him my world, but he wants the moon.

~

I replace the receiver, ecstatic.

'Sanju! Aasha Aunty has come from America. She was my best friend in school, like Joey and you. We are going to see her. She has two children, you can play with them.'

'Will she give me a gift?'

She is back in Madras, visiting her parents. Friends from the age of seven and inseparable through school, we sat together in drowsy classrooms waiting for the last bell to ring, then talked for hours in the evening over the phone.

In the touchingly confident way children predict their future, we foresaw ours. Her husband would be chosen for her. Education limited to a basic degree, she would be wife, mother. Her parents would hand her, cocoon-like, to her husband, let him decide what sort of a butterfly would emerge.

Her future, her happiness, was impaled on the single stake of that mystery man.

I had no such fears. I would soar high above others in achievement, fall madly in love, and have eleven children. 'A cricket team,' I used to say. Maybe one more, the spare.

We meet at a different elevation, both of us resting there, having climbed past marriage and motherhood. We no longer see with clarity the future. What will she teach her daughter about life? I wonder. What picture will she draw for her?

We sit on her bed, regress to protected, happy childhood, the exchange of confidences. Yamini and Sanju and Pranava watch television in the next room—a treat we have granted ourselves.

She has cut her hair boyishly short, close to her ears. It suits her, makes her look very pretty. Her body is wider at the hips, heavier. She uses *surma* instead of kohl. It glistens, a trace of silvery black on the rim of the eyelids. Every now and then, when she calls out to her children, a shade of an accent, a drawl, surfaces in her voice.

The strain of bringing up two children aged six and four, in a tiny flat, all by herself, with no adult company has undone her, she tells me. Rajesh must work to provide for them, and he is away for long hours. She has no babysitter, no time to herself.

From her letters, and our conversations, I can picture her life in America, describe it as if it were mine.

She travels the entire distance to America worried that she will not recognise him. In her mind, a jigsaw puzzle in parts; taller by a head, thick hair, side-parting, dependable fingers, a lean frame, black eyes guarded by astonishingly long eyelashes. Generic, these features do not merge into the countenance of a beloved, her husband. He left just two days after the wedding. She got her visa three months later. Her heart hammers an aberrant song, now pensive, now frisky.

In the flat, a primeval pair, him and her. Shorn of a crowd around them filling expectant pauses, uncertain silences, they now have in excess what they would have yearned for: time alone with each other. There is no family assessing her on the silent scales of the eyes. This is intimacy unrelieved, a solitude too much to bear. And yet, there is honesty and ease in their discovery of each other.

They go for a long walk in the college campus nearby. Ahead, beyond the red brick buildings, within the curving boundary of pale blue water, is a steady sweep of verdant colour: a golf course. If someone took a photograph of the scene just then, she would be in it too. With him. The thought creates in her a sense of dislocation.

A week into her new life, Aasha is left in the apartment to do anything she likes. 'You have to be independent here,' he says. 'Don't cling to me.'

There is little activity that gives structure to her day. In the mornings, the sun is lambent on the left wall of the sparsely furnished living room, moving right before receding at dusk. They do not have a TV; voices stream into the room from the radio. Soon, she listens to every song played, hoping to win the $ 1,000 prize for the song of the day — her dependence is complete.

Rajesh leaves for work early, returns late, taciturn in his tiredness. He is kind, undemonstrative and they grow towards each other slowly. A natural progression, unlike the abrupt way they began to share intimacies at night.

'I miss you,' she writes to me. 'Just to talk about nothing at all.'

Inside the little flat, each sound is discrete, standing apart from the silence around. It offers itself for inspection, naked, unaccompanied, sometimes inviting an unwilling audience; before Rajesh brushes his teeth, he hawks in a manner that she finds unbearable.

On the highway when he drives her to the mall, windows up, the busy world rolls serenely by, soundless, unconnected. Loneliness proclaims itself loudly but is absorbed into the silence. No cattle, no pushcarts, no mongrels, no pedestrians, no pavement stalls, only a silent flow of cold, well-policed order.

She could scream for effect.

He introduces her to his Indian friends. She meets people with whom she has nothing in common, cannot find a friend among them.

She calls me one day, speaks of the shock of encountering a male gynaecologist. It is too late, she cannot leave the room. She feels the insistent pressure of the nurse's hand on her thigh, urging her to behave, to submit. Hot tears slide across her temples until the soft smacking sound of latex being peeled off tells her that it is over.

She sits up, sobbing at the way her body mocked the resistance of her mind. It even mocked its own feeble opposition, permitting an easy entry and a palpation too brief to protest against.

The doctor, Porter, from the badge on his shirt, is exasperated. He is young, blonde. 'I don't understand what the fuss is about,' he says. 'You Asian women seem to have a hang-up about this.'

She cannot bring herself to look at him as she slides off the examining table. Outside, she tells Rajesh that they have to find a female gynaecologist. He must have been taken aback by the unfamiliar assertiveness in her voice.

She is pregnant with their first child, seven months ahead of me. She joins an art class. Two weeks into her first winter there, she can no longer summon the courage to trudge through the snow. The brisk chilling air is so cold she imagines she is trekking across invisible mountains of ice. Tall buildings dwarf trees, reversing the natural scale of things. Bare branches—stick drawings by a child.

It snows steadily for a week.

'What is it like?' I ask. 'Pretty, like in pictures?'

She writes back, 'Only when it is fresh. When it is muddy and turns to slush, then, no.'

Snow changes the shapes of things, hides their true nature, makes everything seem bigger, fuzzier.

Simultaneously, it reduces her, makes her curl into herself, drives happy thoughts from her head. She waits till mid-afternoon when it warms up a little to take a short walk, but when the snow hardens to dangerous ice, she gives up on the idea. The path is too slippery. *What if she were to fall?*

In a letter to me, she describes a moment of beauty. Turning at College Green, she goes up the cobble-stoned path towards Aldridge. To one side of the path are slender trees with a thin, pale bark and small, wispy leaves. They wear ice like a concave sheath of glass. A cold sun is slowly making its presence felt. Pale light catches on the surface of thin stalactites; diamonds glitter on the branches of trees. It is spectacular. She stands a long while staring, forgetting herself in the stillness and the quiet.

Detached from event, days became indistinguishable. Monday through Sunday, looped lazily into weeks, and weeks into cold, bewildering months. She is immured within the apartment.

Her parents are to reach Columbus towards the end of June. Before this prize—the sight of her parents and the arrival of her baby is hers—she has to endure the slow passing of days. Just as she had refused to believe she would live in America until she actually got there—for fear of disappointment—she holds anticipation and joy buried deep within herself, not wanting to tempt fate.

One day, she notices a book on pregnancy given to her a while ago, virgin, stuffed carelessly into torn gift wrapping. She picks it up and begins to read. When she puts it down, the dark smothering cloud has moved, dispersed by a strong, single ray of light. Each day matters. Each day some little part of her child is being formed. With each passing day comes growth and viability. From then on, the book is always by her side as she lives from week to week, waiting to relate the changes taking place inside her.

Her body starts getting heavier, her movements slower, and she is tempted to daydream, wonders what her child will look like, this little being who drums on the inside of her stomach with tiny feet, who goes confidently about the business of making itself grow with minimal assistance from her.

Then the fears come flooding in: *Will she carry her pregnancy to term? Will she survive the test of labour? Will her child be healthy?* She yanks out the frail sapling of elation and stamps on the soft earth of the heart that foolishly nourished it.

There is a lull, between the time the baby flies out of her and the time that she actually holds her in her arms, when she feels she is her old self again. Blown out of shape, depleted, but still recognisable as that young girl, daughter of Shanta and Narayanan, who was given in marriage to Rajesh. She receives her daughter on the length of her arm, is mother.

'Lucky you!' I write. 'You can dress her in silk pavadais, buy ribbons, give her bangles to wear. Imagine, *surma* in her eyes! She's mine, I'm taking her.'

When she has her second child, she looks back at that innocent version of herself in Dr. Porter's office and smiles. Having gone through labour twice, the team of nurses and doctors ranged in a semicircle opposite her, their eyes focussed on that very place, she has lost a certain sense of shame forever. Shame was the last thing on her mind as she fought each wave of pain with her screams, waiting, waiting for the end of it.

And yet, there is the divide of culture. The paediatrician looks askance at her when she says that her four-year-old sleeps with Rajesh and her. *Sleeping is a communal activity where I come from*, she wants to tell him. *What about those infants dying in cribs, left unattended?* A woman is escorted out of a mall for breast-feeding her baby, seated on a bench in the promenade. The security officer has forgotten a natural, imperative function, his gaze irrevocably tainted by a sexual filter. Young mothers from the locality hold a sit-in the next day. There are things to be admired in America.

This time, a boy. She holds him to her breast and is rejected. She tries. Tries again. He will not accept her. 'Must've had a bad mouth experience at the end of labour,' says the nurse. A plastic nipple tricks nourishment into him. A nightmare begins. She expresses milk for him, for every single feed, for six months. She hates the pump, the deep thrill of pain, but she persists.

One child filled her life, two young children possess it. The course of her day is decided by their gentle rhythms, their simple needs: nourishment, play, sleep, play, nourishment, sleep.

'Pranava is so different from Yamini,' she writes, 'It's like trying to move a stone, roll it, with the mind. I think he was born to trouble me.'

Yamini fits herself to her love, to the way she expresses it. Pranava fights it. They are mismatched, mother and son, at a tangent. She takes all of herself, pours it out for him only to find him tipping over the contents with one piercing cry, a blow, 'No!' He does not eat. There is only so much time for a meal, before the next one begins. The circuit of love never completes itself.

In the universal set of possibilities, there is an approach that is right for him. She embarks daily on an expedition to find one with matching serrations. The ideal she gives shape to, makes tangible for him to receive, is rebuffed. Hearing complaint and opposition flung at her continually, she feels ragged. She sees a hand grabbing a malleable head, smashing it nose first against the wall, blood dripping everywhere. It terrifies her. She slaps him hard, instead.

He is so different with Rajesh, she finds it exasperating.

She slides into a depression, hides it from Rajesh. She has learnt him by now, the things that can be said and the things that cannot, the right time to present information. *When she cannot name the source of her despair, what is there to tell him?*

She can no longer summon the will to care for herself. When the children nap, she curls up in a chair, unwashed, her hair in a mess, teeth furry, her mind incapable of cheer. She finds herself sliding, sliding endlessly down a deep, dark well, into nothingness.

Winters are difficult. She yearns to be back in Madras, wants humidity, muggy warmth and the bright dazzle of the unrelenting sun. Sometimes the tears stream down her cheeks and will not stop until she falls asleep, spent. *'Where am I in my life?'*

Half an hour before he is home, she rushes through the apartment in a daze, bathing, combing, brushing, cooking, tidying up.

She begins knitting a sweater for Yamini. But drops several knots, loops the wool tight around the needles and a pale blue rib, hard and unyielding emerges. It ceases to matter then that those rows of knots upon knots should become something. The rhythm of repetition absorbs her, soothes her. The yarn unravels, running over her finger, and the rib grows into a pale blue flag, notched and pock-marked.

Outside, the world offers its many delights to people. Inside, Aasha sits by the window and determinedly weaves a plain and a purl, a plain and a purl, row upon faulty row, wave upon wave...

I call to wish her on her birthday. She tells me that when Rajesh asked her what she would like as a gift, she wanted to say, *'A day off. Be by myself, away from the kids,'* but the thought shamed her into silence. 'I want to leave everything and run away.'

'Me too,' I say.

She cannot return to India until her green card comes through.

She lies heavy on the bed, staring at the boards of the false ceiling, mesmerised. The children are playing ball. Their squeals are remote to her. The flat white surface seems to be very close, the more she stares at it, the closer it seems to be. If it falls on her, she will be flattened, made even of surface, rid of the protuberances that mark her as woman. She cannot move a muscle, the ceiling is on her.

She needs help, tells Rajesh.

'What do you want me to do?' he asks. 'How can I help?' His eyes are moist. Already, he does his share of chores, plays with the children when he comes home, but that time passes swiftly. He draws her into his arms. She can hear the rapid, exquisite flutter of his heart. There is nothing she will refuse him, not even at night when she is tired past absorption and his fingers tug her shirt free at the waist, glide over her back.

Words elude her, the lived experience of misery charted from day to day banked in a place beyond words. Just as she has forgotten the intensity of the terrible pains which stopped the instant the baby was out of her, she is left cradling a sense of exile and despair in her heart but cannot describe the progression of feelings that led to its birth. *Why is she so miserable?*

In America—air, trees, buildings, people, malls, roads, food—she explores the meaning of these words anew. At a certain level, she takes these things as given, allowing them to form the background against which Rajesh and she lead their life. Driving a Ford or a Honda, commuting two hours to work, drinking Pepsi from chilled cans, picking up a pair of Levi's at the mall, eating at McDonald's or Taco Bell, inserting countless quarters into slots for candy, laundry, pop, these everyday events are part of the ordinary in America.

The memory she carries of a place where these things were inaccessible until recently, endows these random acts with significance.

The ordinary turns magical, viewed in the context of that memory, of that background. There is a semblance of unreality, of living in a dream, a welling sense of prosperity; she has left behind the unremarkable life in Madras, escaped the tenor of the lives of those left behind.

And yet, there are expensive saris lying in her suitcase, unworn. She looks at them and wonders, *'What for?'* There is elaborate gold with which she garlands herself once a year, a gaudy weight on her shoulders. The community events they attend—Diwali, Puja, Independence Day—seem tinged with desperation. The streets outside are empty of festivity; to feel a quickening in the pace of life surrounding oneself, is celebration itself.

There is nothing in her life that makes a bridge from present to future, nothing to look forward to, from one day to the next.

She wants to point out a roadside shrine to Pranava, an auto-rickshaw to Yamini. *Kaaka*, cow, green PTC bus, *mallipoo*, she wants them to know these things, place these words on their tongues. That big tree over there, she cannot name it. *'Where am I in my life?'* She has ushered two living beings into a world she cannot gloss, negotiates her way with no map, her childhood far away from her.

She tilts into the solidity of his body. *Be here with me,* she wants to tell him. *Don't leave me alone all day. Please.* She weeps, shaken by ugly, rasping sobs. He takes a week off from work. On the Monday of return, she clings to him in panic, limbs shivering. 'Don't go.' He takes her to the doctor, who recommends a psychiatrist.

She looks at me through the wash of saline—her eyes always reddened quickly—waiting for me to speak. In school, she would cry for every little thing, I was the stoic one.

'I have caught up with you,' I say. 'This past year, I have put Sanju to bed and cried, every night.' I tell her that I understand, talk to her through glass. The drugs are efficient, ruthless. She remains fragile, given just so much space for herself by a protective transparent wall.

This is how we cope: she, buffered by Prozac; I, on the seat of prayer.

~

That divinity abiding in every being in the form of compassion,
I bow my head before Her, again and again and again
and yet again.

That divinity abiding in every being in the form of contentment,
I bow my head before Her, again and again and again
and yet again.

I call out to Sanju.

'Come, come quickly! Show me your hands.'

He hides them behind his back, turning his entire body from side to side. 'No.'

Why did I ever use this word?

There is a brown smudge on his lips that proclaims him a thief of chocolate.

'Please.'

'Why?'

'Please!'

He grants me the favour and stretches them in the front, palms down. I hold his hands in mine, turn them palm upwards so they rest like two small flowers on a broad leaf. I immobilise him with my knees. Now he can't slip away. He is bewildered. Is this love or a scolding?

'Repeat after me. *Karaagre vasate lakshmih…*'

'Karagre,'

'No. *Kar aagre vasate lakshmih…*'

'Karaagre vasate lakshmih,'

'Good! *Karamoole saraswati …*'

'Karamoole saraswati,'

'*Karamadhye tu Govindaha prabhaate karadarshanam.*'

'Karamadhye...Maa, what does it *mean*?'

I tell him about the deities reigning on his palm.

'Even in my left hand?' he asks. He looks down and sees the radiant goddesses seated on enormous lotus flowers, pink for Lakshmi, white for Saraswati. He sees Krishna leaning against a single cow surrounded by a herd. He sees an owl, a swan, a *veena* and a flute, all dwelling in the infinite space of his little hands.

~

'So this is your son?'

I nod. We have been ambushed by someone who was my junior at college. A flashy square of gold on his finger announces that he is now a manager, has status. His shoes are scuffed, dull. We stand one after the other at the pay counter of a grocery shop, there is no way of avoiding conversation by interrogation.

'How old is he?'

'He will be six soon.'

'Five years and ten months,' chirps Sanju. He walks in circles around me, his hand trailing my knees, makes of me Shiva-Parvati, all three worlds. 'And five days.'

'You stopped dancing when he was born, right?'

I nod. I know where this is heading.

'No one could believe you would give it up and just sit at home. I remember seeing your photograph in the papers. Plus you studied architecture. All that education wasted! Your seat in college could have been used by someone else. How come your husband allowed you?'

I choose to remain silent. The man accepting cash is taking forever to serve the person ahead of me. He painstakingly counts a little pile of coins.

'So are you working somewhere? Have you taken up a job?'

He has touched a raw nerve. I am ashamed by a momentary misgiving abnormal to me, being made to feel worthless.

I stare at him, fire in my eyes.

'I am a mother,' I say, 'forty-eight hours a day.' I put my hand on Sanju's head, ruffle his hair. 'This is where I have given my time, my energy. When I look at him, I see my years growing before me, my harvest.'

I hold his gaze until he drops his, adjusting his tie nervously. This is a man who has children, a wife!

~

The story of a mother and her daughter.

As far back as the link of matriarchy can be traced with living stories, Rukmini had a daugher, Uma. Uma had a daughter, Visalakshi. Visalakshi had a daughter, Ambika. Ambika had a daughter, Aditi. When Ambika pulls a soft, smooth Kanjeevaram burnished with gold out of her cupboard, she takes the name of Uma. When she slides a pearl ring onto Aditi's finger, she tells her about her great, great-grandmother Rukmini. Aditi wears their jewels on her wrists, drapes their favourite colours, their stories around her body. She has one child, a son.

My earliest memory—of a home in Santhome, by the beach, her presence within. Yellow curtains, cane furniture and the day when a man made spangly dots out of old *zari*. There was a door that opened onto a winding spiral staircase and was used only by servants. That strange man sat by the open door on the landing, half inside, half outside. He crouched over bellows and a flame for a long time before handing Amma a little glass vial filled with powdered gold.

'For bindis,' she said to me. I must have been four.

The story of my birth, which she never tires of relating, and of her travails as the mother of a newborn, are all linked to this block of apartments. In the rainy season, herds of goats would take shelter beneath the staircase and when they left, small black pellets would be strewn all over the place letting off an awful stench. Sometimes, she would hear the sound of a kid bleating for its mother, and thinking it was her baby, run to check on me.

This is what Amma remembers. It is raining. She is alone in a new city. Jayaram is not in town.

The first twinge in her swollen belly, and she makes her way to the nursing home in Mylapore, refuses to leave even though they tell her it is too early, will take another day. Her older friend Shubha, a mother at fifteen, already a grandmother, comes to help her through the night. The eminent lady doctor whose nursing home it is, delivers the baby close to dawn, after a long precarious labour.

She has no experience of babies, has not even held such a tiny infant before. When she sees the thin fluid dripping from her breast, she weeps. How will it nourish the child, this watery substance? Shubha is immensely amused; she laughs, 'What did you expect, pudding?' In the morning, Shubha leaves to go home, have a bath and breakfast.

She has the baby for company. A daughter finally, after years of wanting. She places a finger under the bump of a nose—*is she breathing? Does she know how to?* Jayaram walks in later, saying briskly, 'Let's go,' missing completely the gravity of what she has gone through.

Once home, she sees even more clearly her isolation. The tumult of romance led to a marriage against the wishes of her parents; they broke ties with her. There is no one to ease her into motherhood, remove her anxiety. In the block of flats where they live, the kindness of neighbours helps her through the early days of weakness, caring simultaneously for the baby. When she looks at the child, her hair so thick, perfectly manicured nails, something deep within is satisfied, made calm. Joy wells in her. In time, a rapprochement is made; her parents' home open to her once more.

It is a funny thing about names. All the time the baby was growing in her, the only names she could think of were Ashok, Vinayak, Murali. Jayaram takes one look at his daughter and names her Aditi. Even as the baby grows, it has a personality of its own. She is clean, does not dribble and smells delightfully fresh at all times. She will not eat, though.

Some days, there is more Farex on my mother than in the baby. She nurses me for more than a year until the doctor scolds her. She did not know when to stop, she tells me.

I was an adventurous toddler, passed from one pair of adult arms to another, forever disappearing into others' homes and she would have to follow a trail of friendship to find me.

There is a photograph of her that I loved to look at as a child. She is standing in front of a house being built, the home we moved to near the River Adyar. She wears dark glasses. They make her look mysterious, svelte. I am in the photograph too, hidden in her ninth-month enormity, behind her starched *sungudi* sari. That bare, unpainted construction is transformed by her into a lovely home, an imaginative garden planted around it. My childhood unfolds within that secure, airy expanse.

A frizzy-haired, rounded figure in a sari. Throughout the day, I follow her in and out of the kitchen, to the lawn where she has her tea every evening, to the dining table where I try to follow my parents' conversations, offering a word now and then. Her *pallu* has myriad uses, primarily a hand towel for me.

At night, she settles me on top of her stomach and pats me to sleep. There is a single lullaby she sings, and it is only when I have grown a bit that I realise that the words 'fan sees' are really one word, 'fancies'. Until then, I sleepily imagine a fan with eyes, seeing angels.

I remember a night when there were guests, the house aglow with laughter. Long past my bedtime, she took me upstairs. She patted me for a while, thought I was asleep. I waited until she had reached the door, turned the handle and then sang, 'Ma!' She retraced her steps, to my elation.

As I grow older, the beds acquire a mosquito net. I am tucked into a square tent, while she reads a book beyond the veiled dimness. The night is never scary, never faced alone.

When I return from school at three in the afternoon, I fly up the stairs, bang on the door of her bedroom. She emerges, warm from siesta, in her petticoat and blouse. I am enveloped by her, welcomed home.

The universe created for me is a loving one. I am its focus of delight. Hugs, kisses, demonstrations of affection from both parents. *Surely, everyone has this?* When a friend of mine tells me that her father does everything for her, is both father and mother, explained to her the facts of life, I am not able to comprehend that distant mother. When others tell me of discord with their mothers, of mistrust, I am not able to understand it, so completely aligned with her am I.

Precious scene: Appa is returning from a trip. We are to go to the airport to receive him. I cannot wait till it is time. What will he bring for me? I seize a pencil, write about a zooming car, begging it to take me to the airport quickly. Amma reads it and is thrilled. 'You wrote a poem!' she exclaims. The way she says it, the way she puts away the pad of paper with care, I perceive that it must be a wonderful thing to write a poem. Later, she applauds every poem of mine that is published.

It is she who places me in the care of the guru who taught me dance. At the time of my *arangetram*, we mull over every detail: the costumes, the jewellery, trying to extend a small budget to include as much as we can.

And so through the growing years, an abiding presence, the visible cause of my existence, firm, loving, fun. In the deep waters of memory, certain moments surface, glistening like fish-scales—the day I discover a smear of mud in my panties and rush to her, worried how it got there; the day she takes me shopping for my first bra; the day I wear a sari for the first time; one particular afternoon, when she sat behind me for an hour, combing a mess of knots out of my thick waist-length hair, trying not to hurt.

Through adolescence into college, she makes seamlessly the transition to a friend. When she remembers her childhood, she thinks of her majestic but distant parents, parents who provided generously but were meagre with love. She makes up her mind that she will bring up her daughter differently.

She talks through her worries, hides her concern in solemn practicality, says that even if I have an untimely pregnancy, there still might be a way of managing it—she will pass the baby off as her child! I giggle when she says this. At eighteen, it is too far away for me to imagine.

Now, at thirty-two, I appreciate it differently.

She talks of change, her growing up from a shy girl to a capable, independent person; of her disenchantment with marriage: 'The only reason one marries is to have babies'; of the neccessity of financial independence: 'Sex and money, two things you never discuss in public.' She examines every nick life has marked her with to warn me. I am bathed in lavish streams of motherly advice.

'I've learnt this the hard way, *kanna*, no one told me all these things. I'm telling you so that you'll benefit; at least you won't make the same mistakes.' That statement, a preface to all our dialogues, a sad lilt stealing into her voice, two deep lines creasing the space between her eyebrows like a tiny caste-mark. In college, I am envied for having a 'cool' mother.

When she stretches out her hand, she reaches magically through transparence to touch the inner me. There is nothing I cannot tell her, nothing that she does not tell me. 'Even if you get into the worst sort of trouble, come to me. We will sort it out to together. Somehow.' 'Somehow' is the operative word, a mother's guarantee that accompanies me to college abroad, keeps me safe and carefree no matter where I am and in whatever circumstances. Somehow. There is no freedom I find abroad that my parents have not already given me.

She writes to me almost every day. Appa though is not regular with his letters. It is pathological, he says, about his lazy reluctance to write. When he does write, it is like unexpectedly finding the end of the rainbow in the mailbox.

The sight of her handwriting on the Indian aerogramme does strange things to me. It establishes me elsewhere, tells me that I am not in Madras, and yet it binds me with the happenings at home, the mundane things I am anxious not to miss. I remember standing bare-headed in razor-sharp wind, flurries of snow drifting silently about me, opening her letter with stiff hands. I entered a nebulous world, neither here nor there, my eyes travelling along an inky filament of love to the spacious rooms of my home again.

When I had left Madras, she had played out the umbilical cord; her womb, the calm centre from where I set forth bravely across the world. Degree completed, I tug on it and am rapidly reeled back home again.

The fine granules of the past having fallen through in a heap, I have four complaints in my sieve. She once gave me raw egg disguised in my milk. She forced me to drink three glasses of milk everyday until college. She sold my beloved yellow five-gear bicycle, when the roads became unsafe. Three complaints actually; I can't find the fourth. Her sincere, unshakeable defence, 'It was for your good.'

Just before I get married when she sees my mind waver, she brushes away my doubts.

'Look at me, I married a philosopher. You tell me, in all these years how many stimulating, intellectual conversations did we have? Mostly, your father would complain about ants on the dining table or why his dinner was not ready on time.'

A little more than a year later, she holds her grandson in her arms, in the very nursing home where a daughter was born to her and a circle completes itself. A boy, the surprise of it! She had chosen pink, with lovely smocking on it, certain it would be a girl.

She looks down the ill-lit corridor, glancing at the closed doors of rooms but cannot discern where exactly hers was.

The next generation having arrived, there is a gap between us on the subject of motherhood.

It is a strange irony of life. She spoilt me with her love, in the sense that I could never bear to accept the idea that there might be uncaring mothers. I spoilt her in the same way: she looks at Sanju now and is unable to see how a child might not be in exact harmony with its mother, configured to match her energies, her need for space.

> *Greater than ten teachers, is the preceptor; greater than ten preceptors, is the father; and greater than ten fathers, is the mother. The mother is greater than even the earth. There is no guru greater than the mother.*

> *Because she bears, she is called* dhatri: *for giving birth, she is called* janani; amba, *because she nourishes the limbs; and* virasu *because she carried child with courage. In rearing with love and care, she is* sushru; *the mother is one's own intimate body.*

—The Mahabharata

~

Something has happened. The top of a rented *shamiana* stretches parallel to the road, making an open two-walled room of it where it turns at the corner. A couple of rickety folding chairs, the metal denuded of paint, occupy one side of the road. No coloured bulbs, no banana leaves arching over the narrow path leading to Palani's cottage.

It must be a funeral.

The pen, put to other uses, looks unkempt. The buffalos are no longer tethered there. Thayee is nowhere to be seen. *Could it be hers?* No, it cannot, I reassure myself. *Why, I just saw her in the morning!*

The news spreads casually: Palani is dead.

He had been sick for sometime. They sold the buffaloes to pay the medical bills. Yama slipped his noose tightly around him and then reeled in the thread of life with slow deliberation, causing Palani much suffering. All agree that he was punished for the way he treated his mother.

Has someone told Thayee? Does she know?

It takes only a minute to visualise the procession that will leave sometime in the afternoon. Palani's body wrapped in white, the face covered, brought out and placed on the bier. The head placed to the north, the legs pointing south. The sound of wailing, the excited chatter, the squeals of children, all being hushed momentarily.

Women, standing like pillars in the doorway of their homes that open directly onto the street, watching, secretly glad for the elevated view. His neighbours, the dhobis, the brick-layers, the auto-rickshaw driver, gathered in an awkward group, slightly bemused by the finality of death, but alive to the excitement of the event.

Some of them will jostle and push to get near the body, to place a garland of tuberoses on it, the flowers appearing yellowish against the dazzling white of the cloth. And then a baby might cry or a dog bark and the spell of silence would be broken. A car might reach the corner and the driver realise his mistake. He would have to stop the car, forced by circumstances to watch.

Then, when the moment can be postponed no more, the drummer will start: *dhum ta takra, takra taaa-dhum ta takra, takra taaa,* wearing the heavy drum like a bag on his shoulder. The pall-bearers will lift that body of insignificant weight and move out of the shade towards the cremation grounds, the bier tilting this way and that, their faces solemn, absorbed. Ahead of them, someone will scatter petals of flowers—rose, marigold, jasmine—on the road. And the sweet strong perfume, now the smell of death, will ride on the breeze for a mile.

Where will Thayee be?

Will that bold lump of flesh, the daughter-in-law, let her near? Or will she stand at the threshold of some stranger's house, an onlooker at her son's funeral procession?

~

It is bedtime. I capture Sanju and make him sit by the sink so I can wash his grubby hands and feet. The water that runs off him is black. He has long legs, a long skinny body. The food I have fed him with such trouble has gone toward making him taller not wider. His bottoms are the roundest part of his body, satisfyingly round.

'Do you know that a baby's feet are the cleanest feet in the world?' I ask him. 'That's because it cannot walk. You had pink feet as a baby. I used to kiss them. Now look at them! All yucky bucky.'

I pretend that I am trying to kiss them but for the dirt. He giggles. He loves stories about himself.

'You must always wash your hands with soap. Especially before eating.'

'Why?'

'There are bad germs everywhere. So we have to clean our hands.'

'You said *Bhagavaan* is in everything, then how can they be bad?'

~

When Thayee bends her head to get up, or nods, her long ear lobes swing gently. At some point in her childhood, her ears would have been pierced and a neem twig inserted in the still bleeding flesh. Over time, pith would have worked the perforation wider until the day, when her parents could afford it perhaps, a solid, distinctive gold earring, with curious angles and curves, weighed it lower, distending the lobes to her shoulders.

One auspicious day, she would have looked into the mirror and seen herself assume bridal garments, jasmines and the glimmer of gold. It is a fact that at another moment, forced on her on a day long past, Thayee renounced colour forever and practised a sad alchemy, converting those huge nuggets of gold, *paambadam*, into food. The mutilation is irreparable.

~

The clouds in the sky are like snow-covered mountain peaks. There is a thin edging of gold around them; the sun has not yet set.

I am in the car, parked near the vegetable stalls on a main road. Amma is shopping, followed by Sanju who tugs at the edge of her sari from time to time, twisting himself into it.

'A joy,' she had said.

Near me, three women selling strings of jasmine and marigold, a man selling bananas. They have set up makeshift tables, planks of wood nailed roughly together, just off the road. When the police come to chase them away, they quickly dismantle their portable shops.

There is the ebb and flow of traffic. People are walking, crossing roads, buying things, planning their lives. Nimble cyclists swerve past heavier vehicles, madly ringing their bells, and hungry cows wander about. Together they spin a colourful web of sound. Dusk is upon us. Everything, as far as my eyes can see, everything pervaded by the same consciousness— I imagine how it must be. It is difficult.

A luminous, powerful philosophy. When that which is subtle, immense, intangible is limited by name and form, it coalesces into something that is tactile, tangible, sentient and sometimes only too human: the shape of a mother or perhaps that of a small, adorable infant.

I try to see a glow near the heart of all beings. A light, a spark, a flame divine. The women, the men, householders, passers-by. Far away, the ragged urchin near the garbage pile. The placid animals, the drunk fallen insensible at the bus stop. The woman sitting on a step, cleaning her ear with a feather. Ahead, the boy leaning from the footboard of the bus. I imagine their bodies fading, becoming incandescent, a perishable frame for that eternal, glowing light. One, all one. The trees like spiders at the base of the mirror of sky, the space holding us, this earth. One. And me, the last pearl on that single thread. The differences we pride ourselves on, essentially an illusion. Details, mere details.

Sanju hops into the car and in the expanded second before the spell is broken, I perceive a flame in the pure centre of his heart.

~

We are illuminated. Without announcement, without ceremony, men from the public works department throng the street, measuring inches and charting height. By evening, at irregular intervals, there are tall f-shaped lamp posts flooding the road with a strong golden light. The upper branches of the trees are revealed, light pools in certain leaves, gifting them their green, and darkness loses its mystery in patches, is altered, made safe. Our unknown street is exalted, made alike an avenue. The occasional neon light remains, cold and diminished.

Beneath the neem, a filigree of leaf-shapes spreads itself over the warm bed of lit road. Thayee need no longer fear the invisible creatures of the dark, she is secured by light. She picks up a champak, contemplates that yellow-pink flower awhile before bending her face. Its nectar enters her.

~

That divinity abiding in every being in the form of a mother,
I bow my head before Her, again and again and again
and yet again.

That divinity abiding in every being in the form of delusion,
I bow my head before Her, again and again and again
and yet again.

Tall, brittle, leaf-screens fence the area cleared for the new house to be built, preventing the curious onlooker from peering inside. A small cottage made of thatched leaves has been erected to one side, where the gate used to be. A man and his wife will live there as caretakers till the construction ends.

The slender woman is visible there at various times, chopping onions or stirring something in the pot. Her cooking gives off a strange, pungent aroma; it celebrates the wedding of sun-dried chillies and a fish from the sea.

Thayee has reclaimed the space under the neem. Her possessions are now reduced to the bucket, the roll of cloth and two stainless steel vessels.

~

It is past afternoon, not yet dusk. The watchman of the new flats waves a hosepipe tamping down the dust on the road, releasing heat. Thayee sees an opportunity. She ambles into the jet of water and is refreshed. Drops of water bounce off her, glinting like gold beads.

He laughs.

She raises her hands, trying to catch water. He is gentle at first, then becomes more fierce in the way he directs the flow at her body. It is a fight now. But Thayee is happy to lose; she has made him give her a bath.

Gradually, the trees yield their green to twilight and become black, bushy shadows. Sanju will have to be prised loose from the set of children playing by the hand pump and taken home. As I walk past the doorsteps of homes, the wind carries gossip.

Here, in this home, tomato rasam is being made, in this one, the scent of talcum powder tells of a bath and fresh clothes, and here, I can see the evening lamp lit and incense touching the senses calm.

~

I read to Sanju from my Amar Chitra Katha on Hanuman—his favourite. A priceless treasure that survives my childhood, kept safe in plastic folders. It is his now. I cannot wait for him to enter that magical world by himself.

We bound across the ocean in one giant leap and enter the palace with him. It is night in Lanka. Sleep is upon everyone, the guards as well. We tiptoe past Ravana, terror pounding within us.

'Maa. Maa.' He nudges me urgently. 'Does Ravana have one *big* pillow or ten pillows under his heads?' His voice echoes loudly in the palatial bed chamber.

It is a question I never thought to ask myself. There is no time to check. We scurry past, lest Ravana wake up, raise a tousled head, or maybe ten!

~

Did Vivekananda ever mention the devotion Adi Shankara had for his mother? It is a story in which he is sure to have found a personal resonance. I ask Appa.

He is in his study. Behind him is the huge wall of books bright with random colours. Two shelves are filled entirely with the literature of Ramakrishna and Vivekananda. On some days, he travels, sitting on his cushioned chair, to Dakshineshwar. On others, he enters into long conversations with Vivekananda.

An hour later he calls to me.

'Look!' he says with great excitement, 'in his *Letters*, there is one addressed to Sara Bull, dated January 17, 1900.' He begins to read:

> *It is becoming clearer to me — that I lay down all the concerns of the Math and for a time go back to my mother. She has suffered much through me. I must try to smooth her last days. Do you know, this was just exactly what the great Shankaracharya himself had to do! He had to go back to his mother in the last few days of her life! I accept it. I am resigned... Then again, this is coming to me as the greatest of all sacrifices to make, the sacrifice of ambition, of leadership, of fame... But then, it is now shown that — leaving my mother was a great renunciation in 1884 — it is a greater renunciation to go back to my mother now. Probably Mother wants me to undergo the same that She made the great Acharya undergo in old days.*

He turns the pages of the book, glancing at the letters and finds what he is looking for.

'About two months later, in March 1900, he again wrote to Dhiramata, his name for Sara Bull,'

All my life I have been a torture to my poor mother. Her whole life has been one of continuous misery. If it be possible, my last attempt should be to make her a little happy. I have planned it all out. I have served the Mother all my life. It is done; I refuse now to grind Her axe. Let Her find other workers—I strike.

'In the Mahabharata, Aditi, there is this one *shloka* which is incomparable. It applies to Vivekananda. Vyasa says, "Leave *dharma*, leave *adharma*; leave both truth and untruth. After leaving both truth and untruth, leave *that* which enabled you to leave them. Then take one last step—leave the notion that you have left anything at all." That was Vivekananda, the living Vedanta.'

~

I find that Thayee has been attended to already. She is busy eating, stuffing large balls of rice into her mouth. Since she cannot sit cross-legged, she squats at mealtimes, stretching her hand down to the food or raising the vessel to the level of her chest.

The lady, whoever she is, has taken some trouble over Thayee's lunch today. Two appalams, fried in oil, lie on a piece of plastic close to her feet. She breaks into one of them and a crisp golden sun disintegrates into tiny chips. On that square transparent material, blue-black from the road beneath it, there is also a small portion of mango pickle, the oil escaping from it in a red viscid stream.

I gesture to her to accept what I have brought.

She has no water for the ceremony of washing her hands, nor does she have another dish. I watch her get up, and seeing the effort it takes, it seems to me that I have troubled her more than I have helped. She enters the gate behind her.

While waiting, I feel an abrasion on the steel plate where my finger rests against the side. Tilted upwards, it catches light. There, on the circular band of the raised rim, I find a cluster of dots in the shape of alphabets, my parents' initials and the day they were married, chiselled on this basic necessity of everyday life.

With her moist, polluted hand Thayee breaks off two broad leaves from the widow's garden and holds them, one overlapping the other, supported by her palm. I arrange the food in the centre of the leaves. At least, I know she will have her dinner today.

~

The soft clang of a brass bell. The suggestion of a heavy, ponderous movement in the interval between the next note. A single clang again, the sound suspended above ground. Almost certain now, I run to the window. My heart leaps. Wanting to surprise Sanju before he sees it, I lift him onto my hip and rush outside, swimming through waves of strong afternoon light.

We are late already; it has passed by our house and moved on, a loud tinkle accompanying every majestic step it takes. Sanju gasps, wriggles out of my embrace and dashes forward, tremendously excited. 'Maa, *paaru!*' he cries. Everything he sees must be reflected in his mother's eyes as well.

The huge oval bottom shifts sideways and subsides under the loose, shabby purplish-black skin. The tail, absurdly disproportionate to the size of the body, is like a long-handled brush swinging in the air. Ahead, a group of women wait, offerings in hand. Sanju, impatient, dashes back to me, grabs a handful of kurta and impels me forward with all his strength.

We hurry to the front. Three other children dance around it with all the excitement of wonder.

A housewife in a light blue cotton sari steps forward hesitantly. She holds aloft a bunch of ripe, yellow bananas. The trunk sways drunkenly forward, wet lips open. The woman cringes, laughing nervously in discomfort, and steps back, withdrawing her hand. The bananas are gone though, lifted off her palm and conveyed swiftly to the mouth that is hidden behind the tapering trunk. A vulnerable mouth, unprotected by tusks.

A bulky iron chain is placed around the middle of its body, and a rusty padlock at the end of it. The chain is not tight but rests so close to its skin, its massive underbelly, I wonder if it is comfortable. The bells dangle from the chain, one on either side.

An ornate decoration adorns its forehead all the way to the fan-like ears. Drawn with chalk, the effect is pleasing— pale violet, pistachio green and rose pink filling the white outline, colours that are cheerful against the blackness of hide. A line curves away from the main pattern to end under the serene, watchful eye, emphasising it.

Another woman offers money. The mahout speaks his secret language and the trunk veers to the other side, searching for her palm. The woman places the ten-rupee note in the small cup it has made of its snout and it vanishes between the lips even as he playful trunk is lifted over her in benediction.

Head bowed, shoulders hunched tensely, as though in expectation of a falling axe, she accepts the gentle blow that blesses calmly enough.

I am empty-handed, I realise but there is no time to run inside.

They are moving already. The children follow, catching up with it to run alongside till the end of the road, and I shout after Sanju to be careful. I forgot his slippers in the hurry; it is two thirty and the tar must be hot, but he is oblivious.

The crowd does not move away; it isn't an everyday happening after all. We watch as long as we can, our gaze travelling gradually from a height down to the level. There is a sense of blessedness, for, the auspicious sight can only be a promise of good things to come. From this distance, the mahout seems small and yet, for all his apparent poverty, a man on top of the world.

Later, in the evening, Sanju and I walk down our street on the way to the market. Past the bend, we emerge on the stretch that leads to the main road. There are gigantic mounds of dark green waste on the road, undigested fibre still visible amidst the substance. Sanju tugs at my hand and asks me what it is. I tell him.

'So big! So much?' he asks me, his eyes wide with curiosity.

'It's a big animal,' I say to him, 'Do you know what it eats? Sugarcanes and bananas and grass and jackfruit…kilos and kilos of them.'

He is silent the rest of the way, understanding scale this vividly perhaps for the first time.

~

Assuring my jumpy nerves that silence is not ominous when he smiles his way through sleep, I uncap the pen. Paper receives the burn of ink, mates silently with it.

In the green eternal forests of the *Chandogya Upanishad*, I meet a woman who lived almost 2,800 years ago. I admire her greatly, this brave mother...

It is dusk. There is a shifting haze of dust at the very edge of the village. A boy of tender years leans against the mud wall of his home and watches the cows return from grazing. He knows at last what he wants. He has spent a great deal of time thinking about it. He is ready to accept the austere discipline enjoined on a student, ready for any hardship that might come his way in the course of his studies.

For a guru, he has decided to approach *Rishi* Gautama, the noble and discerning sage, to accept him as his student. One small detail remains though. There is something he needs to know that only his mother can tell him.

He finds her in the garden, plucking jasmine buds. They will open soon and their fragrance will permeate the air.

'Maa,' he begins.

'Look how many I have!' she says excitedly. 'Enough for a long garland.' She walks towards the entrance of their home.

'Maa,' he says, slipping his hand in hers, 'I have to tell you something.'

She puts away the basket of flowers and draws him into her lap, secretly amused by the serious tone of his voice.

'I want to become a *brahmachari*. They say Sage Gautama might accept me as a student, but I don't...' he stops, his brows creased, then asks, 'what is my *gotra*?'

His mother replies immediately, with great dignity. 'I do not know, my son.' There is no hesitation. Her gaze is direct. She looks into his eyes and says, 'When I was young, I worked as a maid in many homes, moving about a lot. That is when I had you. So I do not know to which family you belong and, therefore, not even your *gotra*.'

The boy's face falls.

Without knowing his lineage, how can he present himself before the great *rishi*?

'However,' she continues. He raises his eyes to hers and sees in them the deep and limitless ocean of love. 'However,' she says, 'my name is Jabala. And you, my son, my only child, are Satyakama by name. Therefore, you may call yourself Satyakama Jabala.' Satyakama is happy.

He approaches Gautama, himself the son of Haridrumat and says, 'I wish to become a *brahmachari*. May I become your student, Sir?'

The revered sage says, 'To which *gotra* do you belong, gentle youth?' They are in a clearing, thick around them the forest.

Satyakama says, 'I do not know to which *gotra* I belong. I asked my mother. She said this in reply, "When I was young, I worked as a maid in many homes, moving about a lot. That is when I had you. So I do not know to which family you belong and, therefore, not even your *gotra*. My name is Jabala. And you, my son, my only child, are Satyakama by name." I am, therefore, Satyakama Jabala.'

Gautama then says, 'None but a *brahmana* could have made it clear in such a way. I will accept you as a student. You have not deviated from the truth.'

In time, Jabala's son Satyakama himself becomes an enlightened sage. The *Jabalopanishad* is attributed to him.

It is one o'clock at night. I switch off the lights, pause at the bathroom window and see that Thayee is not able to sleep either. She lies on her back, on the small rectangle of cardboard, covered loosely by the same cloth that she drapes over her body during the day.

It is hot, there is no breeze.

Thayee waves a fan slowly, parting the air in a moving arc, a motion that must retrace itself over and over again, for, whenever she stops, the air will press back thickly upon her, just as rain claims the space cleaned momentarily by a windscreen wiper.

~

That divinity who pervades everything, presides over the senses
and the elements five,
to Her I offer my salutations.

That divinity who pervades the entire universe in the form
of consciousness,
I bow my head before Her, again and again and again,
and yet again.

The doorbell rings twice, urgently.

Who could it be?

We are not expecting anyone. It is close to eight o'clock.
I am in the middle of feeding Sanju his dinner. I stuff a large
bit of chapatti into his mouth to keep him going.

'Stay here,' I tell him and hurry downstairs, skipping
two steps at a time, sticky fingertips closed like a bud. No time
to wash my hand.

'*Yaar?*' I say by way of precaution, the memory of the
thief still alive. There is no reply. I can hear a shuffling sound
on the other side of the door. With my left hand I draw aside the
curtains of the window near the door and peer out. The porch
light is on. I cannot see anyone in the free space between the
car and the doorstep. I lean further to one side, and see a naked
arm a little above the ground.

Thayee! *At this time?*

She gets up as I open the door. The cloth she is wearing
is threadbare, like a fabric woven from dust. 'What's the matter?'
I ask her, wondering what it could be. She smiles when she
hears my voice.

'Do you have any food left?' she asks, the gaping toothless mouth and the angle of the head conveying her request more forcefully than the soft tone of her voice.

My stomach lurches. There is nothing readily available to give to her. We do not eat rice at night and she cannot manage chapattis, probably does not even like them. And yet, in all these years, this is the first time she has taken the extreme step of ringing the doorbell to ask for food. And, even in doing this, she asks, simply; I have never heard her beg.

How can I disappoint her?

'There is no rice, Thayee,' I begin...

'Maa!' He screams, 'Maa?'

'Coming baby,' I shout back, 'Gimme two minutes!'

After a difficult pause, trying to remember where I had reached in my thought, I ask, 'Will you eat chapattis?' I have to shout here, stress the syllables in a different way so she will understand: 'Sapp-paati...'

'No,' she says, shaking her head. 'No teeth left. Am deaf as well and can't see since the day he hit me.'

'Maa!'

There is only one thing to do. 'I'll cook some rice for you,' I say. 'Don't go wandering off. Stay here and I'll give it to you when it's ready.'

'*Ayyo!*' she is shocked. 'You don't have to make it for me! I'll manage. I just thought...' and she turns away facing the darkness beyond the porch.

'No! I mean it. You just stay here quietly. It won't take long.'

'No. No. Why should you?' she shakes her head and then her hands vehemently to show she does not want it, and we are in the middle of an argument. She has reached the gate. The new streetlights are not working. The night has acquired a certain strangeness; the houses lining the road and the road itself, lit inadequately by a pallid neon tube light, look like something one has lost temporarily and found again.

'If you go away...' I have to threaten her with my disapproval before she subsides to the ground, sits on her haunches, waiting.

'Maa...!' I can hear him all the way down here. I'll have to wash my hands now.

In the kitchen, I put the rice into the cooker and rush upstairs to feed Sanju. The chapattis and vegetables have become cold.

'Who was it?' asks Amma. I tell her.

Later, as soon as I can open the cooker, I mix the rice with some curds taken from the fridge, but the rice is so hot, it absorbs the coldness of the curds. I measure the salt into it carefully.

At the gate, Thayee has fallen asleep. I shout out to her, and she stares at me with an angry frown, the light from the distant neon lamp post glinting eerily in her eyes. The rice is very hot, though; she cannot eat it immediately. She lies down on the ground again, and I am forgotten.

The neem is a vast, still shape, part of a larger, shapeless immensity. A light breeze is blowing. A half-tablet of silver gleams in the sky. The fragrance of the raat ki rani pervades the darkness like an intense, unrelenting ache.

I turn to go inside.

Warm, yellow light streams invitingly from the open window, the staircase inside is visible from this point. An antique five-wick lamp dangles from the lowest part of the banister where Amma has placed it, framed within a single span of the window-grill.

~

A phone call from Murthy.

After five sentences of inconsequential chatter, I wonder what it is he is leading to. He announces that he has been asked to remain in France another year. The additional responsibilities will require more travel. We are not to disturb ourselves. He will spend his earned leave with his parents and brother. Only after he has put down the phone do I realise that he did not ask even to speak to Sanju.

Amma reads my thoughts.

'What is your problem?' she says. 'He does not drink, he does not smoke, has no bad habits.' She notices the nap of dust on a rosewood table and wipes it clean with her *pallu*. 'He is not having an affair. I know youngsters like you want romance but, he does not make *any* demands of you! You are free to do what you like, bring up your child the way you want to. Why break it?'

~

'Sakha saptapada bhava...'

With these seven steps, let us be friends
I seek your friendship. May we never deviate
from this friendship.

Astonishing, the sense of equality implied in these words, the acceptance of the other's individuality. There is a measure of self-assurance, a standpoint of composure from which the one approached the other. Mother, grandmother, aunts, none of the elder women in my family have ever used the word friend to describe the conventional attitude towards a husband. And yet, each one of them had participated in a rite where these verses were sung; this is what they had agreed to in that ancient, perfect language.

~

'Maa.'
'Umm.'
'Maa!'
'Umm.'
'Maa!'
'What?'
'Why doesn't Shiva *Bhagavaan* change his clothes always?'

~

It is Sanju's birthday. I turn six as a mother. I place a piece of cake in his mouth and feed the living god.

Life does not happen to plot. Everyday life, largely uneventful, flows on, and it is the personal routine that gives shape to time, holding up the fine collapsible fabric of day and night. Reality does not immediately lend itself to meaning that is complete, definite, its edges sealed. When one looks back over a period of time, however, happenings arrange themselves to suggest a story, the story of one's life.

A child occupies immense space in its mother's life. Of all intimacies, perhaps this is the most intimate, to share a body for nine months. The day my child was born, that day I too was made anew. *Dwija,* twice-born. In placing one's child at the centre of one's life, does one displace oneself? Does the progression from being self-centred to being selfless as a mother, necessarily involve a loss of self?

One moves from lower truth to higher truth, not from error to truth.

Is *avidya,* recognised only in retrospect? One knows oneself but partially. Two steps behind reality, I am still trying to understand the changes that Sanju's presence have wrought in my life, a life that is still to be lived, still an unfinished story.

In June, he will go to school full-time.

School is a place invented by tired mothers.

~

To truly see the divinity immanent in each one of us is perhaps very difficult. To see it in one's child is to make a beginning.

Vivekananda's anguish at what he saw in his travels across India made him declare:

> *No religion in the world preaches the dignity of humanity in so lofty a strain as Hinduism and no religion on earth treads upon the neck of the poor and the low in such a fashion as Hinduism.*

To dissolve the rigid shrouds of race and religion, caste and gender that imprison a human being and make free, visible, the divine within is to make a beginning.

Our true shining selves are a part of the immense oneness of the universe. In the nature of our inner, *true,* selves, we are

One, but we see people and judge them from the outside: poor, rich, beautiful, ugly.

What is the true nature of this One self? Truth, Consciousness, Bliss. How empowering, how freeing, to look beyond the confines of one's own history!

To know the One self in every Other is to make a beginning.

I have made such beginnings.

~

No one has seen Thayee. She has been missing for a month. It takes a while before people realise this. Even I, erratic in generosity, have not noticed. There is no way of knowing whether she went to her other sons. Perhaps she fit herself into a void somewhere else.

On this, her street, the last of the vacant spaces was built up, the widow found new tenants and Thayee could take shelter nowhere, except under the neem. She had become frail in the preceding months. No longer could she climb over locked gates or lower herself into garbage bins. Once, I heard her ask a passer-by for money.

So many were the times she scared me, lying on the kerb, with her lifeless appearance. Then she would turn or straighten a leg and the knot of worry would come undone.

I search for a woman with white hair, dragging herself about in a garment the texture of dust. An unlettered woman, a woman leaning against nothing but God.

I find a broken bucket, neem flowers on the ground and an absence.

Had there been a body, had there been the finality of death, then it would have fed the very elements once her voice had entered the fire, returning what had first proceeded from them — her breath mingling with the air; her eyes reaching the brilliant sun; the mind speeding towards the full, effulgent moon; hearing to all the directions; the self dispersed in ether; the hairs of the body to the aromatic herbs; the silver mass on her head to the trees; and fluids, blood, to the waters of the earth. The name alone would have remained.

Instead, there is hope, and its disappointment. On certain days, I look through the gaps in the leaves and for a moment, I think I see her, the rounded fold of dusty garment, the slim, brown branch of the tree her bare arm and my heart skips a beat, but I am mistaken.

~

That divinity abiding in every being in the form of illusion,
I bow my head before Her, again and again and again,
and yet again.

Nectar in the ear

In this flow, the human life,
I believe
the only
moment that counts
is that in which
the delightful deeds
of the boy of complexion blue
are savoured
with devotion ineffable.

— *Krishna-karnamritam, III.34*

References

The following sources were vital for the writing of *Meeting Lives*, particularly for the kind of details I was looking for.

Swami Vivekananda

The Complete Works of Swami Vivekananda; The Life of Swami Vivekananda by his Eastern and Western disciples; *Saint Sara* by Pravrajika Prabuddhaprana; *The Life of Josephine Macleod* by Pravrajika Prabuddhaprana; *The Master as I Saw Him* by Sister Nivedita; *Swami Vivekananda, A Historical Review* by R.C. Majumdar.

Adi Sankara

Adi Shankara, His Life and Times, Discourses delivered by His Holiness Shri Chandrasekharandra Saraswati Sri Sankaracharya of Kanchi Kamakoti Pitha, translated by T.M.P Mahadevan; *The Hymns of Shankara* by T.M.P. Mahadevan; *Sri Sankara: His Life, Philosophy and Relevance to Man in Modern Times* by Dr. S. Sankaranarayanan.

Upanishads, Krishna and Karaikkal Ammaiyaar

The Principal Upanisads by Dr. S. Radhakrishnan; *Garbha Upanishad* – Net Resources, *Srimad Bhagavatam* translated by Kamala Subramaniam; The Krishna Book, ISKCON; *Periya Puranam* translated by G. Valmikanathan; on *Karaikkal Ammaiyaar* – Net Resources.

I am grateful to the following people who spent time in conversation with me, answering my questions: My father, Chaturvedi Badrinath; Dr. S. Sankaranarayanan, Head, Adyar Library and Research Centre; Shri M. Harikrishnan and

238

Smt. Meenakshi about the forests and trees of Tamil Nadu in the 5th Century BC.

The verses from the *Krishna-karnamritam* are based on a translation by Shri M.K. Acharya. I have taken liberties with his translations, modifying and rearranging them.

The passage quoted on Page 89 and page 90 is from *Sri Ramakrishna, The Great Master* by Swami Saradananda.

The verses at the beginning and end of each chapter are from the *Devi Mahatmaya,* as also the verses quoted on pages 119, 120 and 121.

The verses on page 148 and 149 are from Sankara's *Bhaja Govindam.*

The words 'hugs the form of death, embraces the terrible', on page 160, are of Swami Vivekananda.

Translations relating to the *Yoga Vashishtha* on page 164, the Mother on page 212, and Sage Vyasa on *dharma* on page 221, are from *The Mahabharata, An Inquiry in the Human Condition* by Chaturvedi Badrinath.

The words in italics on page 233 *'One moves from lower truth…,'* are of Swami Vivekananda.

The last paragraph of the book is an adaptation of a passage from the *Brihadaranyaka Upanishad.*

Glossary

aapat sannyasa	*sannyasa* taken at a time of grave danger or trouble
abhinaya	emotive expression by a dancer, carrying the audience towards feeling a particular sentiment or mood
adharma	not-*dharma*; disorder; unrighteousness
ashram	hermitage
ashtapadi	a composition with eight stanzas, usually refers to those of the *Gita Govinda* composed by the poet Jayadeva, 12 AD
asura	demons
asuri	in this context, roughly translates to 'demoness'
atman	self
avidya	ignorance of the true nature of reality, false understanding, incorrect knowledge
Bhagavan	God
bhakti	devotion to God
bhava	expression of an emotion rendered while immersed in a state of feeling
brahmachari	monastic probationary; student: the first of the four stages of life
Brahman	Absolute Reality
brahmana	brahmin
chakra	Catherine wheel; firework that spins on the ground
danda-kamandalu	staff and spouted water-pot carried by mendicants
darshan	being blessed by the very glimpse of the deity
daya-dana	compassion-giving of alms
deivame	calling out to God
devas	demi-gods
dharma	that which sustains, enhances and does no violence; order inherent in the universe
diya	clay-lamp

240

gana	certain troops of demi-gods who are Shiva's attendants
gopis	cow-herdesses; milkmaids; Krishna's companions in play
gotra	lineage or clan assigned to a Hindu at birth, based on ancestry sprung from renowned sages such as Kashyapa
getti melam	furious din made at the time of tying the *taali* to scare away destructive forces
gurukula	residence with the guru while studying
Ishvara	Supreme God in the Yoga philosophy
jathi	sequence of pure-dance movements
jiva	living entity
kaaka	crow
kadavale	calling out to God
kolam	design drawn in rice-flour by Tamil women everyday in front of the home
mallipoo	jasmine
mandapam	wedding-hall
manushyatvam	birth as a human being; one of the three things obtained with great difficulty by the grace of God according to Shankara. The other two being desire for freedom: *moksha,* and association with a realised soul
maya	illusion, the veil covering the Absolute Reality or Brahman
mridangam	percussion instrument
mudra	fingers held in a particular position that conveys a certain meaning
nadaswaram	wind instrument
namaskaram	palms joined together in obeisance
ogoru	agarwood incense
pandal	temporary shed especially used for public gatherings
patram pushpam phalam toyam	I will accept a leaf, a flower, fruit or water

	if offered to me with love and devotion, Bhagavad Gita, Ch.9, verse 26
pey	departed soul; word used by Karaikkal Ammaiyar to describe herself; ghost
prasad	food offered to the gods first and then eaten
rakhodi	circular ornament placed at the back of the head
rishi	sage
Sanchita karma	sum of all *karma,* good or bad, accumulated over past lives, that is carried through to future lives
sandhya	rituals performed at the critical juncture of dawn and dusk
Sankhya Yoga	two among the six systems of Indian philosophy
seva	service
shamiana	marquee
shloka	verse in Sanskrit
sringara	erotic love
surma	cosmetic for the eyes
swara	musical solfa notes
swayambhu	self-existent; self-created
talai saman	jewellery adorning the head of a Bharatanatyam dancer
tali	auspicious symbol of marriage worn around the neck by Tamil women
tambura	musical drone instrument
thali	complete meal served at one go in a plate with raised edges
thinnai	stone seating provided on either side of the front door; characteristic feature of traditional Tamil homes
tillana	musical composition where certain defining syllables such as *ta, tani, tom* recur in a sequence
todapey	broom made of feathery reeds tied together
varnam	particular sequence of music central to the Bharatanatyam repertoire
zari	gold thread

Acknowledgements

Punam Barman for being my Best Friend from the first standard in school.

Mini Krishnan for her generous praise on reading the book and her stern reminders to remain true to its purpose and not change a word.

Jyotirmaya Sharma, Dr. Uma Ram, Christine Luisi, Sushant Sarin, Dr. Meenakshi Tyagarajan and Sunita Rao for reading various early versions of this book and being frank in their response to it.

Dr. Sumita Kale for her frequent requests to send further excerpts from my book.

Corinne Chabert for her generous response on reading my works which served as great encouragement to me.

Dr. K.S. Subramanian for being the wonderfully reassuring paediatrician that he is.

Francesca Patrizi for her great concern and affection.

Dipa Chaudhuri, my editor, for her perceptive remarks and admirable attention to detail while readying this book for publication. Her gift for conversation and the literary tastes we share were some of the happy discoveries made while working with her.

Buwa and Manju Shete for graciously showing me around Buwa's studio in Pune, and for generously consenting to the use of Buwa's painting for the cover of this book.

Satyajit for being so patient while taking photographs of me, including the one in this book.

Vaishali Mathur for her prompt responses and involvement in the preliminary stages of editing.

Navidita Thapa for the vibrant elegance of her design that met and surpassed my expectations of the cover.

Chinmaya, my son, for patiently compiling the words in the glossary.